THE PRIVATE EYE

Nat Craig, London's foremost private investigator, believes in hitting first and pulling no punches, which makes for exciting episodes, including murder, blackmail and robbery, from his casebook. The indomitable Craig ruthlessly tracks down the evil-doer, and each case contains a genuine and logical problem of detection . . .

ERNEST DUDLEY

THE PRIVATE EYE

Complete and Unabridged

LINFORD
Leicester

First published in Great Britain

First Linford Edition
published 2014

A catalogue record for this book is available
from the British Library.

ISBN 978–1–4448–1868–0

Published by
F. A. Thorpe (Publishing)
Anstey, Leicestershire

Set by Words & Graphics Ltd.
Anstey, Leicestershire
Printed and bound in Great Britain by
T. J. International Ltd., Padstow, Cornwall

This book is printed on acid-free paper

The First Case:

The Ash-Blonde

Anyone who knew Nat Craig personally would also know that if they walked into his office they would almost invariably find him with his feet on the desk, tilting his chair lazily backwards in order to obtain a better view of the clouds of smoke which rose to the ceiling from the tip of his inevitable cigarette.

Craig said it helped him to think.

He was tilting, smoking and thinking hard when Mr. Geoffrey Moran rang him up.

'Speaking,' Craig said laconically into the mouthpiece. 'What's on your mind?'

Mr. Geoffrey Moran had plenty on his mind.

He spoke rapidly and nervously for a few seconds and gave Craig his address in Ealing.

'I'll be over. Two-thirty. Hello? Hello?'

The faint click in his ear told Craig that Mr. Moran, apparently having no desire to prolong the conversation, had hung up.

Craig eyed the telephone speculatively for a moment, shrugged and went off to lunch.

He took a tube train at a few minutes to two. He wondered idly if Mr. Moran's abrupt end to his phone call might have been inspired by someone else in the household interrupting him. Someone whom Geoffrey Moran wouldn't want to know about private detectives.

Craig grinned to himself and lit a cigarette. He hoped the Moran family wasn't a large family. The process of elimination could become tedious.

The street was wide and lined with trees that hid the neat houses with their sedate formal gardens from curious passers-by. A few were superior to their neighbours in that they possessed garages. Geoffrey Moran's house was one of these.

Craig walked up the short cement drive and pressed the bell. He pressed it three times before he heard approaching

2

footsteps. A tall ash-blonde opened the door.

'Yes?'

Craig told her pleasantly:

'I want to see Mr. Moran.'

'I am Mrs. Moran. I am afraid my husband has just gone out.'

She had a slightly guttural accent and Craig tapped her as a Scandinavian. The solid type. Cool and not easily ruffled. He raised an eyebrow and murmured:

'Pity.'

'Is he expecting you?'

Craig eyed her and let an amused quirk tip the corner of his mouth. 'I would not have come all the way out here on chance.'

'Well . . . '

The ash-blonde hesitated and her lips widened, showing small white teeth. It was a particularly humourless smile and the scent of some subtle, clinging perfume she was wearing drifted across the porch to Craig's nostrils. Finally, she offered:

'Can I help you?'

'Maybe, yes. Maybe, no.'

Craig unhitched his shoulder from the doorpost where it had been taking a rest and told her who he was. He watched her face, but she didn't bat one of her mascaraed eyelashes. Instead her forehead wrinkled up in a puzzled frown.

'I wonder what on earth Geoffrey would want to see a detective about?'

Craig enlightened her as far as he was able.

'Seemed afraid someone was going to bump him off.'

She stared at him, hesitating. Then:

'Won't you come in?'

'I'd love to,' Craig accepted politely.

She took him through a small hall and held open the door on the right. It was the lounge and ran the width of the house with a bay window at the front and French windows leading into a long rhododendron-lined back garden with a cluster of trees at the bottom.

She picked up a silver cigarette box and offered it to him. He indicated his unfinished stub and watched her as she helped herself, tapping the cigarette thoughtfully on a crimson thumbnail.

4

She appeared to be deliberating on what to say next and Craig was in a singularly unhelpful mood.

'My husband said he was going over to see a friend who lives in the next road.'

She spoke at last, slowly and keeping her voice carefully conversational.

Craig nodded expectantly.

'He knew I was going to be in here all afternoon,' she went on. 'I wonder why he didn't tell me you would be calling.'

Craig suggested obligingly:

'Maybe he thought the idea of a detective around the house would worry you.'

She nodded in agreement.

'I expect that was it. Anyway, if he's expecting you, I'm sure he won't be long.'

Craig grinned amiably. He said cheerfully:

'Don't let's have any misunderstanding about this, Mrs. Moran. I *am* a detective and *not* somebody trying to sell you a vacuum cleaner and your husband is expecting me. He asked me to be here at two-thirty.' He glanced at his watch. 'It's just that now.'

She began a slow smile that indicated she wasn't sure if he was trying to be funny or not.

'It's such a lovely afternoon,' she suggested. 'Geoffrey may have decided to go for a stroll on the way home, which would take him longer.'

Craig eyed her.

'It could work out that way,' he agreed.

There was a pause while she regarded him levelly. Then her face clouded; she crossed to the open French windows and stared out for a moment before turning back with a sudden restless movement.

He thought it was all very nicely timed and melodramatic to say the least of it, and she heightened the effect by twisting her hands together despairingly.

She said, as if she had just come to a difficult decision:

'Mr. Craig I might as well admit it, I'm worried about my husband. He's been so very moody and strange these last few months. It's overwork, but though I — I begged him to go away for a holiday, he just won't move. I haven't told anyone before what I'm telling you because he'd

6

be furious with me. But after what you have said, I mean, that he's afraid someone is going to — to kill him — '

Her voice trailed off, leaving Craig to prompt her.

'You mean he's, shall we say, imagining things?'

'We-ell — ' It was a long-drawn out syllable. 'It does seem rather far-fetched to believe anyone would murder him, doesn't it?'

Listening to the suddenly matter-of-fact tone in the bright little lounge on a sunny afternoon it ought to have seemed ridiculous. Mrs. Moran gave the impression she thought so at any rate. Craig, who looked for trouble, and murder in particular, in the most unlikely places in any kind of weather, smiled.

'But you *are* afraid of something.'

He put the query gently. As he spoke he became aware of a creaking sound above his head. It was so soft even his sharp ears could not be sure of it, but it was always as well to check up. He said slowly:

7

erhaps you don't like being left alone in the house?'

She laughed.

'Oh, no. I assure you I am not the sort to imagine things. My husband is out a lot but it would not worry me even if the neighbours did not live so close to us. I do not feel lonely, ever.'

Deliberately, Craig looked at her. He said blandly:

'I'm glad of that.'

Her mood changed again. She should have been an actress, he thought.

'But you're right, Mr. Craig. I am afraid. Afraid that my husband might do something desperate.'

There was a pause. Then she started nervously as there came an unmistakable noise from overhead.

'One of the windows banging. I think I'll just slip up and close it.'

She hurried from the room and after a moment Craig crossed to the French windows and gazed out at the garden.

He lit a cigarette and blew the blue smoke out into the warm air. Everything was very still and dreamily lazy. A perfect afternoon, and there was a faint hum coming from somewhere which could have had a most soothing effect if only he had had a deckchair, he reflected regretfully.

Craig stepped slowly through the windows and the humming grew in volume. He tilted his head and listened. It could almost be bees busy among the flowers. Only it wasn't bees. A speculative look narrowed his eyes and then a voice behind him said:

'It *was* a window.'

He turned to face the ash-blonde. She was breathing a little quickly.

Craig grinned.

'Oh, those stairs,' he murmured.

'I beg your pardon?'

He shook his head, still grinning. 'It doesn't matter.'

She looked at him curiously, then flicked at a cushion that had slipped down into the corner of the couch.

He realized that everything in the room from the curtains to the walls seemed to match Mrs. Moran. The dress and the shoes and the clasp she wore, and the

...ur scheme certainly suited her blonde sophistication.

Craig told himself she was either out of her element or all dressed up for something, which wasn't an afternoon alone. Or both.

He glanced at his watch again.

'You know, I think your husband must have forgotten me after all.'

'Oh, I'm quite sure he hasn't really,' she protested, and he decided she rose to the occasion pretty well. Then she continued quickly: 'But if you'd rather not wait, I will tell him you called and I expect he will get in touch with you again.'

Craig nodded.

'I am a busy man.'

She flashed him a smile.

'I realize you must be,' she said. 'I can't apologize enough, but it just shows the state of my husband's mind these days. I do hope it hasn't inconvenienced you too much?'

He told her: 'Think nothing of it.'

He followed her through the hall to the front door. In the porch he turned.

'Your husband has a car?'

She hesitated. 'Yes . . . ' And her eyes flickered past him towards the gates at the end of the drive.

Craig said slowly:

'Maybe he's gone farther afield than into the next road to see a friend? Shall we take a look-see at the garage?'

She shook her head. 'If Geoff had taken the car I should have heard him leave. I'll tell him you called.'

'You said that before. As for hearing him leave . . . I don't think your hearing is as good as it could be.'

Her eyes flew back to his face.

'What do you mean?' she demanded jerkily.

A humourless smile crept across Craig's mouth.

'I hear a buzz,' he said. 'Don't you?'

She looked at him, puzzlement in her eyes.

'I — ' She broke off and tilted her head back. She seemed to be genuinely trying to catch the sound that he had noticed in the lounge.

'Yes — ' she said at last. 'Yes, I do hear something.'

'Shall we go along to the garage?' he said again.

Without a word she led the way along the gravel path at the side of the house. The humming noise grew louder as they walked. He heard her catch her breath in her throat and she turned quickly towards him.

'He must be in there,' she cried, indicating the garage ahead of them.

The doors were closed and Craig moved fast. One shake was enough to show that they were not only closed but well and truly locked.

'The key?' he rapped.

She was frightened now. He could hear her breath coming in staccato gasps.

'There's only one — behind the front door.' She gulped and stood staring at him as if the power to move had deserted her.

'*Get it.*'

She turned and ran then, while the hum persisted steadily behind those locked doors.

She was back in a few moments and Craig pushed her away as he threw open the doors and the choking smoke from the exhaust billowed out at them.

'My God!' choked Mrs. Moran.

Craig fixed a handkerchief rapidly over his face, ducked into the garage and reached the car. A figure was slumped over the steering wheel. Craig leant across and cut the engine.

'Geoff! Oh, Geoff!' The woman was sobbing, all her stolid calm gone to the four winds. 'Is he dead?'

He rasped at her:

'No one could sit that out and live.'

Craig coughed as the deadly carbon monoxide fumes caught at his throat and lungs.

The air in the garage was clearing as he lugged the body out of the car and dragged it outside. Mrs. Moran clutched at the dead man's coat hysterically.

'You can't do anything,' Craig told her briefly.

Whimpering and crying his name, she helped him carry Geoffrey Moran into the house. They dumped him on the couch and Craig looked on bleakly while he watched her push the cushion under her husband's head.

'It's no use!' she moaned. 'It isn't any use!' And then she promptly collapsed on her knees beside the couch.

Craig regarded her for a brief moment. He said:

'Get a doctor. Not that he can do a thing. Then phone the police.'

'Police . . . ?'

She raised her head from her arms and looked at him wide-eyed through a tangle of ash-blonde hair.

He nodded, unperturbed.

'It's murder. But, of course, you know that.'

His words seemed to slap her in the face, and she looked up at him as if he had been a ghost.

'*What are you talking about?*'

She moved towards him. She looked as if she was about to spring at him.

'Take it easy,' he grinned at her amiably. 'Or I am liable to forget my manners. And when I sock people,' he added pensively, 'they have a habit of staying socked. Personally I don't think you killed him.'

'No?' she jeered. 'Thanks for nothing! Who did, Mr. Clever?'

But her eyes were guarded and frightened.

Craig cast a fleeting glance out at the garden:

'Outside,' he said crisply, 'there isn't enough breeze to stir a leaf — so that was not a window banging. I should say it was your accomplice — boyfriend, maybe — hiding upstairs.'

She gasped. He smiled almost apologetically and went on:

'These modern houses are the devil. They relay every sound.'

'You . . . '

She was on her feet facing him and her face was livid. Craig's eyes hardened and he went on relentlessly:

'Your boyfriend no doubt knocked out hubby, then dumped him in the car with the engine running. You were hoping to get away with a suicide set-up. You'd overheard him phone me, so you didn't wait. You didn't dare, it would have been a bad mistake to have let him have that little chat with me. Only thing was,' he said slowly, 'you made a mistake of another kind. One of you locked the garage and returned the key.' He nodded towards the front door. 'Which was silly. If the key was there, how could your husband have locked himself in? It couldn't have been taken without your knowing . . . In your own words, you have been here all the afternoon.'

For a moment there was silence while they stared at one another, then her eyes suddenly widened and shifted to a spot over his shoulder.

Craig spun on his heel, ducking his head to one side — and the heavy poker that the curly-headed young man had aimed at the back of his neck whistled harmlessly past his ear.

The woman screamed:

'*Jim!*'

'Hallo, son,' said Craig chattily, and whipped his fist into the newcomer's stomach, bending him up like a jack-knife.

Curly Head gave an agonized grunt and lurched forward. Craig grabbed him with his left hand and pushed him back to arm's length. His right fist draped itself shatteringly on Curly's jaw. Craig released him and let Curly Head sink gently to the floor.

'And now, Mrs. Moran,' Craig said genially as he put his foot firmly on the poker, 'shall you call the police? Perhaps, after all, you don't feel up to it, so I will.'

And Craig picked up the telephone.

The Second Case:

The Warren Street Alibi

When the door clanged behind him and he stood on the right side of the prison walls for the first time in three long years, one thought lay uppermost in young Sammy Ryan's mind. It was to find, as soon as possible, the man who had been directly responsible for his wearisome sojourn as guest of His Majesty's Government.

That man's name was Craig.

But Sammy's aim was not as had been many others who had found themselves in the same unfortunate circumstances. He was not nursing a revengeful hate in his heart — on the contrary, his emotions towards the private detective were of a hopeful, friendly nature.

He had a healthy enough outlook to realize that Craig had borne him no personal animosity. Craig had been responsible for getting Sammy a stretch simply as a result of his investigations of that particular case and, in fact, had felt sorry for him. Sufficiently sorry to promise to see that Sammy would be all right on his release — that was, if Sammy's protestations when he went in, that he wanted nothing more than to go straight, still held when he came out.

Three years behind bars having convinced Sammy Ryan that above all things the straight and narrow was the path for him, he now sought Craig's redemption of his earlier promise.

Nor did Nat Craig fail him.

So, when one evening Sammy's wife came round with the news that old man Robinson had been done in and the police were holding her husband, Craig was interested.

Mrs. Ryan said tearfully:

'I just don't know what to think — only it wasn't Sammy that did it. He wouldn't. Why should he when you were so kind in getting him a job and everything? Why should he kill Mr. Robinson?'

She was sitting on the edge of a chair in

his office with a damp ball of handkerchief screwed in her fist. Craig placed a hand on her shoulder.

'It's all right, Mrs. Ryan. It hasn't been proved he had anything to do with it yet.'

She dabbed at her face with the handkerchief. 'But you know the police. They'll be thinking it was him because of him being put away last time, but it wasn't — '

'They can't pin anything on him on account of that,' Craig soothed her. 'I'll go down and see how the land lies.'

Her eyes were shining with tears and gratitude.

'It'd be ever so kind of you. Poor Sammy'd be that glad to see you.'

Craig said: 'You slip home and I'll have a chat with Sammy.'

When she had left, Craig made his way to Robinson's the newsagent in Warren Street where he had found Sammy Ryan a job. It seemed unlikely that Sammy would do such a crazy thing as murder his employer just when he was getting along steadily as an honest citizen. Craig seldom misjudged his man and he didn't like to think that he had made a mistake this time either.

He found Inspector Hooper plus his sergeant and the fingerprint and photograph boys already at work when he reached the little shop. The police surgeon, having expressed his opinion that the deceased had been shot in the back of the head from a couple of yards' range, had departed.

Craig gazed mildly round the scene from the doorpost.

Inspector Hooper hadn't expected to see him so soon and Craig suspected he didn't look overjoyed at his appearance at that.

'What do you want, Craig?'

'Just thought I'd come along,' explained Craig pleasantly. 'Sammy's a sort of protégé of mine you might say. I feel quite responsible for him.'

His gaze swept the shop.

The Inspector murmured to the rabbit-toothed individual that he had been talking to before Craig had appeared on the scene.

He turned back to Craig. 'He's in the sitting room at the back,' he said shortly, 'waiting to be taken along to the station.'

'Sammy never carried a gun in his life,' Craig offered mildly.

The other shrugged.

'Maybe he's been seeing too many gangster films since he came out. He had a gun this evening all right.'

'Yes,' chimed in Rabbit-tooth. 'He was carrying it when I grabbed him.'

Craig turned slowly and raised an inquiring eyebrow. The Inspector sighed.

'This is Mr. Benson,' he said. 'Mr. Robinson's brother-in-law.'

'How nice,' murmured Craig.

Benson gave him a stiff nod. 'A terrible business,' he offered. 'Lucky I hung on to the chap.'

Craig was interested.

'What happened?'

'I'd just gone out for a few minutes to telephone my wife — this telephone is out of order — and I heard the shot,' explained Benson. 'I came back immediately, of course, and was just in time to spot Ryan dashing out of the shop. I grabbed him and held on while I yelled for the police.'

'Motive: robbery?' queried Craig.

The Inspector nodded vigorously.

'No doubt that was it. Only Mr. Benson's arrival scared him off.'

'I'm sure it did,' said Craig feelingly. He encountered a nasty look from the Inspector and added: 'What does Sammy have to say to all this?'

Hooper looked surprised.

'He denies it, naturally.'

Craig nodded calmly. He drew out his cigarette case.

The Inspector shook his head but Benson helped himself and Craig gave him a light.

'Do you have far to go?' he asked conversationally.

Benson gazed dumbly at him and Craig explained: 'In words of one syllable, where do you live?'

'Chorley Wood. Why do you ask?'

Craig looked amused.

'What are you worrying about?'

'I'm not worrying!' snapped Benson.

'Not worrying when your brother-in-law has been shot?' Craig reproached him. 'I merely asked where you lived. Do you mind?'

'Of course I don't mind. Though what

business it is of yours exactly — '

The Inspector cut in grimly:

'Mr. Craig has quite a way of not minding his own business.'

'So it seems,' Benson said. He shot Craig a look from under his brows.

'And I thought I was being friendly,' remarked Craig imperturbably. 'Where did you make your phone call from?'

'Call box on the corner of Warren Street.'

'It's quite a bother getting through sometimes.'

'I had a bit of bother myself,' Benson admitted. He was thawing slightly.

'I noticed that call box,' Craig said as if the other hadn't spoken. 'It's got no light.'

'That's right. Kids must have bust the bulb or pinched it or something. Lucky I'd got some matches. It took me about five minutes dialling Toll — used up half a box finding. 'T' and '0' and 'L'. My wife heard the shot, too, as a matter of fact. She thought it was some car backfiring.'

'Must have been some shot!'

'It was a heavy calibre army revolver,'

the Inspector put in. 'Makes a noise like a cannon.'

Benson went on:

'I realized it was no car though, so I ran out. As I said, I got to the shop just in time to catch Ryan — luckily.'

'Very luckily.' Craig shook his head sadly. 'I wouldn't have thought it of Sammy.'

The Inspector said:

'Looks as if you misjudged your man.'

Craig didn't answer at once but drew at his cigarette. Then he asked quietly:

'Can I have a word with Sammy?'

The Inspector nodded.

'If you think it worth your while.'

Craig disappeared into the back sitting room.

He found Sammy Ryan sitting on a hard chair and not feeling too happy about any of it, but he was pleased to see Craig.

'Glad you come,' he said. 'You been wonderful, but wot's the use of me saying anythink? I done time and that's marked me.'

Craig eyed him through a cloud of

cigarette smoke. He made no comment.

Sammy jerked his head morosely towards the shop.

'It's an open and closed case to them. But I never done it, honest. Though I can say so 'til I'm blue in the face. I got no proof — nothink, but I swear I never done it.'

'Neither have they got sufficient proof — yet,' Craig told him.

Sammy Ryan turned towards him eagerly.

'You believe me, don't you?' Then he slumped again. 'But wot's the use. They'll cook up somethink, you wait and see if they don't. They got enough to work on and then they git a clever chap along in court and you see wot 'appens — '

He broke off expressively.

Craig said:

'What's your story, Sammy?'

'Ain't no use my telling 'em that, Mr. Craig.'

'I'm not asking you to tell them. I'm asking you to tell me.'

'All right, Mr. Craig, all right,' whined Sammy miserably. 'It was like this, see. I had to go out for Mr. Robinson, up to the Euston Road. When I gits back he's in the shop getting ready to close up. Well, I was just going through the back when I hears this here gun go off. Terrific bang it makes,' added Sammy reminiscently. 'Nearly scares the hide off me and for a moment I was all confused like. Then I rushes into the shop and sees the old man laid out on the floor, it didn't half give me a turn, I can tell you. I kicks up against the gun and without thinking — honest, Mr. Craig, I didn't know wot I was doing — I picks it up and before I knew wot was happening I dashes full tilt into Mr. Robinson's brother-in-law who was coming into the shop. He grabs 'old of me and 'ollers for the cops — '

Sammy broke off and brushed his hand across his face.

'About what time did this happen?'

'Must have been round about six. Like I said the old man was getting ready to shut up shop.'

There was a silence for a moment while Craig eyed him bleakly. Then he observed shortly:

'Not much of a story you've got there is it?'

'You're telling me,' the other blurted out bitterly. 'But it's the truth, Mr. Craig, every word of it s'help me if it isn't. I never done it, I tell you, I never done it.' His voice trembled off into a long groan. 'But I reckon I know when my goose is cooked.'

Craig looked at him speculatively for a moment, then he said:

'All right, Sammy. If that's your story, you stick to it.'

Sammy nodded gloomily.

'I shall have to. Being the truth there ain't no other I can tell now. Wish there was.'

Craig smiled grimly and left him.

When he returned to the shop Inspector Hooper greeted him, somewhat heavily sympathetic.

'Pretty thin yarn, don't you think, Craig?'

'Pretty thin, Inspector.'

The Inspector went on:

'Afraid he's for it this time. Frankly, I'm sorry. He was doing well in this job here. And with him getting married and all that, I thought he really meant to settle down. Must be disappointing for you.'

Craig's reply was stony.

'Could be.'

The Inspector was starting to say something, then he broke off. 'What do you mean, 'Could be'?' he growled.

Craig didn't answer. Instead he turned to Benson.

'I imagine between you, you and your wife must have a pretty good idea what time the gun went off?'

Benson blinked at him and caught his sagging lower lip between his protruding teeth. He said slowly:

'I don't know about my wife. Naturally, I didn't wait to ask her, but I daresay the police can check it up anyway. For myself, I should say it was about six o'clock.'

Craig murmured:

'I had a feeling you'd say that.'

'What is this?'

Inspector Hooper sounded irritable.

Craig drew deeply at his cigarette and let the smoke trickle dreamily out in a blue ribbon to the ceiling before he answered Hooper. When he did his voice was icy and there was a tenseness about it that had not been there before. It had the effect of making his listeners feel slightly uneasy.

Suddenly he swung on Benson.

'What were you after?' he snapped. 'Did you want to move in on your brother-in-law's business?'

Benson's face remained a blank. Only his pale uninteresting eyes appeared to glint a little.

'Me?'

'Yes, you!' rapped Craig. 'Come on! We want to know all the story, you're going to have to spill it sometime. Did your wife put you up to it, or was it your own smart invention?'

A spasm of movement passed across the other's pallid face. There was a muscle working round his mouth. He said nothing but only gaped at Craig. He seemed incapable of speech.

Inspector Hooper moved forward quickly with an exclamation. He glowered at Craig:

'What's on your mind?'

'His bright little alibi,' Craig told him brusquely, indicating Benson with a movement of his head. 'Which, Inspector Hooper, I am about to blow to bits.'

Craig turned to Benson smiling affably.

'And after all that trouble you took too, telling us how you had had such difficulties dialling toll by torchlight to speak to your wife at Chorley Wood!'

'What are you talking about?' muttered Benson. He gave an impatient shrug. But his hands were shaking.

'It was very convincing,' Craig congratulated him. 'Except that you can't dial toll from a public call-box!'

'Whassat?' spat out Inspector Hooper, his chin stuck forward.

'Try it sometime,' Craig chided him gently. 'And see what you get.'

As he finished speaking Benson made a sudden swift movement.

But Craig's foot shot out and caught Benson neatly on the shin.

'Panic,' Craig murmured, glancing down at the sprawling breathless figure at his feet. 'You should never panic, never try and run for it. Makes everything look so much worse. Now,' he added. 'Had you merely said in the first place that you dialled 'O' for operator, you *might* have got away with it.'

The Third Case:

The Threatening Letter

The man next to Craig smacked his lips, put down his half-empty glass and said across the bar counter:

'Single-'anded today, Boss?'

The landlord of the Rotunda Arms nodded. He wiped his moist brow with a tattooed, muscular forearm and smiled.

'Yes, it's Eddie's afternoon off. He'll be back this evening, though.'

The other chuckled. He winked knowingly.

'Taking one of his blondes to the pictures, eh?'

'Shouldn't wonder. A lad for the girls is Eddie . . . Same again, Mr. Craig?'

Craig slid his glass over and glanced round the crowded bar.

Most of the customers were enjoying a quick one before hurrying across to the Rotunda Theatre where the matinée was due to start in a few minutes.

The landlord fixed Craig's drink and answered further inquiries coming across the bar after the absent Eddie. It seemed the young barman, with his ready cockney wit, taste in startling tie-pins and inevitable cigarette, was something of a favourite with the habitués of the little Shaftesbury Avenue pub.

Craig lit a cigarette, then glanced at his watch.

As the result of her phoning him that morning, he was due to look in presently on Sarah Lane.

He'd read about the anonymous threat to kidnap the blonde, pulchritudinous Sarah Lane before she'd phoned him. He'd put it down to a bright idea thought up by her over-enthusiastic, if not altogether original-minded, press agent.

When she told him it wasn't any publicity stunt, she'd had the letter all right, he'd told her maybe wasn't it merely some harmless crank, with inhibitions the way cranks have, loosing off a little steam?

She'd said to him, her voice cool in his

ear over the wire:

'You could be right, Mr. Craig. All the same, I'm taking it seriously. The idea of someone, cranky or not, trying any funny business has practically no allure for me. Come and see me during my matinée this afternoon.'

Craig still didn't think it was the sort of business he wanted any part of. Actresses were not his favourite type of client — tricky to work for, he'd usually found them, un-businesslike and unreliable.

'Why don't you get Scotland Yard in?'

'One thing I don't want is police fussing around. I'm told you're a good private detective, Mr. Craig, and I think you could settle this quietly without any trouble.'

Maybe this time it would be different, Craig thought. Besides, he hadn't been entirely unsusceptible to the flattering intonation in her delightfully husky voice. Added to which, she was a star all right and should be okay from the money angle, and he liked to eat.

He knocked back his drink and went out, the landlord calling after him: 'So long, Mr. Craig,' for he was not entirely unknown in those parts.

A minute later he was leaning through the cubbyhole inside the Rotunda stage door. The doorkeeper looked up from the racing news and regarded him aggressively over his steel-rimmed spectacles.

'Well, if you've got an appointment with 'er, you've got an appointment with 'er,' he muttered.

'What's on your mind, Fred?' Craig asked.

'Things is a bit 'umpty,' the other grumbled through his soup-strainer moustache. 'Miss Lane's only just come in, which means she'll be late, and besides . . . '

'This kidnapping threat?' Craig suggested.

The other snorted.

'It isn't that. It's — well — ' He lowered his voice confidentially: 'It's her carrying on with Mr. Barry, and his wife in the show, too. Oh, Miss Lane don't mean no 'arm, but with Mrs. Barry being the jealous kind . . . Anyway, I'll tell her you're here.'

He lifted the internal telephone off its

hook. After a few moments Fred replaced the receiver, shaking his head.

' 'S funny,' he muttered. 'She *should* be there.'

Grumbling, he shuffled off, beckoning Craig to follow him.

They went through double doors and across the back of the stage. The orchestra was tuning up; stagehands padded around in last-minute tidying-up before the curtain went up. They made their way through the gloom that was cut by blindingly glaring beams of light from the lamps round the stage.

As they reached the door on the opposite side of the stage, a large, distraught woman burst out on them.

'Police — ! Quick, the police — '

'Wot's up, Mrs. Abbott?' Fred demanded.

'Miss Lane — ! Miss Lane, she's unconscious! She's been attacked — !' the woman gulped.

'Cripes!' observed Fred inelegantly and turned to Craig. 'Looks like a job for you, Mr. Craig,' and hurried after Mrs. Abbott.

As they gained the dressing room, Craig noticed something glittering up at him just outside the door. He made a quick movement and slipped it into his pocket.

★　★　★

It was the same evening. Place: the Rotunda Arms.

The man next to Craig set down his beer, wiped his mouth with the back of his hand and turned from his evening paper carrying the story of the Rotunda robbery.

'Wot I says is,' he declared, 'wot does she want with all that jewellery? Fair asking to 'ave it pinched, I reckon.'

Craig regarded him thoughtfully and nodded, then glanced again at Eddie. The young barman caught his eye and came from the other end of the bar, grinning at him perkily.

'Same again, Mr. Craig?'

The man was burbling in Craig's ear:

'Lucky she didn't get herself done in. I see she was 'alf strangled, but she come round all right. Who d'you think knocked off 'er sparklers?'

He stopped talking to look at Craig expectantly.

'Yes Mr. Craig,' Eddie said, handing him his drink. 'Who did?'

Craig smiled back at him genially.

A little later found him once more leaning casually through the cubby-hole of the Rotunda stage door.

'Perlice don't seem to have no clue, Mr. Craig,' Fred told him gloomily. 'Only thing is, it must have been someone in the theatre. Who else could it have been? No one who I don't know come through here this afternoon — '

'How about when you took me along to the dressing room?'

'Perlice asks me that, but you remember I left you when you went in with her dresser — Mrs. Abbott — and got back here to find the call-boy keeping my chair warm for me. He hadn't let any strangers through. And even if he had, 'ow could they have got out — without me seeing 'em?'

Craig gave him a bleak stare and a little later took his unhurried departure.

Big Ben boomed midnight as, in

answer to his ring, the woman opened the door. She regarded him with some suspicion. Then, when he told her who he had called to see, just for a little chat, she said:

'He's only just come in.'

She held the door wider for him.

'Thanks,' and he followed her along the dingy hall.

'Visitor for you . . . ' she called and he went in, closing the door behind him.

'*What d'you want?*'

Craig took something out of his pocket and threw it on the table between them.

'Found it outside her dressing room this afternoon,' he said through a puff of cigarette smoke.

'It don't prove a thing. I could have lost it there last night, or — '

'If you had, the cleaners would have swept it up before the matinée.'

The other started to say something, then broke off, inarticulate.

Craig paused to survey the tip of his cigarette. 'I didn't connect it with you first time,' he murmured unhurriedly. 'Then, you see, Fred was dead sure no stranger had gone in or out of the stage door at the time of the robbery and the penny dropped. You *wouldn't* be a stranger to him. He was used to you going in and out with drinks. He never thought of you. That's what you counted on, just as you counted on that crank's threatening letter putting them off your track. And of course Fred wasn't to know it was your afternoon off.' He indicated the imitation bit of jewellery that winked up at them. 'Tonight, it wasn't in your tie . . . '

There was silence in the room.

Craig's voice was almost gentle.

'Well, Eddie?' All his perkiness gone, Eddie fingered the place where his tiepin had been.

'All right,' he said, suddenly caving in. 'I'll give myself up. I got the stuff here . . . '

They went along together.

The Fourth Case:

The Odd Composer

Apart from the fact that she was one of the loveliest girls he had ever set eyes on, Kay Martin's story, whatever it added up to, made a change from the usual type of tale brought into Craig's office.

She walked in through his frosted-glass door early one afternoon and Craig, encountering her smile, decided that it was a beautiful day.

'Won't you sit down, Miss — er — ?'

'Kay Martin.'

Her voice was in keeping with her face.

He grinned back at her and pushed over his cigarette case.

'Have a cigarette, Miss Martin, and tell me all about it.'

She bent her head to his lighter and exhaled the blue ribbon of smoke slowly. 'Now that I'm here my story seems even sillier than it did downstairs.' She looked at him apologetically. 'But I'd love your opinion anyway.'

'I'd love to give my opinion, anyway,' he replied promptly.

She rested one gloved hand on the edge of the desk in front of her, undecided how to begin.

'I was on my way from the café,' she said at last. 'I was going back to the photographer's where I work — I model, by the way — and I happened to pass your office. I thought perhaps you might be the right sort of person to come and see.'

Craig took his feet off the desk. 'You were right. I am,' he agreed.

Her violet eyes flickered.

'I was having lunch,' she went on, 'when this old chap came over to my table. He made me a quaint little bow and told me how he had seen me there several times without presuming to speak to me until today, when, apparently, he felt he had to.'

Craig nodded. He could imagine her smile of tolerant amusement and calculated that it could hardly be a new experience for her to be stared at — or spoken to — by roving-eyed types. No doubt the old boy had looked pretty harmless to her.

'The old wolf,' he murmured.

She laughed.

'I don't think so. Just rather arty. He had a lot of white hair and carried a wide black hat.'

'An artist who thought you might give him that inspiration stuff, is that it?'

She shook her head.

'Not exactly. You see, he was a composer. That was the line he started on. He — he said, though, that a face of my particular beauty usually inspired painters so that they felt that they must reproduce it on canvas. Then he went on to explain that he was a musician and he knew my face could inspire him in his latest composition. It seemed he was pretty desperate for inspiration. Frankly I decided he was merely a bit crazy.'

'Oh, I don't know,' Craig smiled at her. He was thinking he might easily get the urge for inspiration himself if she stayed around for long.

'I don't think you're taking this very seriously.'

She crushed out her cigarette in the large ashtray at her elbow and pushed back her chair. To Craig it looked as if she was about to terminate the interview. He said quickly:

'What name does the old boy go by?'

She looked at him thoughtfully. Then apparently relented.

'Julius Denby.'

She stared expectantly at him.

'Well?' he said.

'Nothing. Only he told me as if it ought to have some special significance. I'm afraid I'm not very musical but I thought the name might ring a bell with you.'

Craig told her cheerfully:

'I'm not very musical either.'

She admitted:

'I didn't respond at all. Anyway, after beating round the bush he mentioned this symphony that he is supposed to be composing. He said he believes it is going to be his greatest work. An idea to show human nature in all its moods, and that sort of thing.'

'Dangerous,' Craig commented, tipping back his chair.

She laughed.

'Isn't it? He told me with the greatest pride that he was going to call it 'The Symphony of the Human Heart'. And did he sound pleased with the title.'

'Sounds very nice.'

'Well, it appears there is one part of the music which he just doesn't seem able to get. He has been working at it for over a week and it still has the poor old thing baffled. He even admitted to me that he was on the verge of giving the whole thing up as hopeless. I suppose he is temperamental and throws moods if his work doesn't fall into place as it should, and then — '

'And then he saw you.'

'And then he saw me.'

She smiled at him with a glorious lack of conceit.

Craig nodded. He said:

'And how exactly does the old boy think you can help him finish his little piece?'

'He wants me to go along to his studio this evening.'

'Where is this studio?'

'Bloomsbury. All I have to do is just sit around while he stares at my face and gets the right inspiration so that he can go ahead and finish off his masterpiece.' She halted and looked at him appealingly. 'At least, that's what he said, but it sounds fantastic.'

Craig shrugged.

'I've met a lot of far funnier things in my line of business. Does the idea of going there alone make you nervous?'

She made a little flutter with her hand, and added:

'I forgot to tell you his housekeeper will be there to watch over me.'

'But you're still nervous.'

She hesitated for a fraction. Then nodded.

'Silly, isn't it? I wouldn't have given it a thought but — well — '

'Well?'

She said flatly:

'It's easy money.'

'You would be crazy if you were doing this inspiration act just for the love of his art. How much did he offer?'

'Twenty pounds. And twenty pounds is twenty pounds to a working girl.'

Craig agreed.

'To anyone, twenty pounds is what you said it was.'

'I'm glad we're in harmony over that. I felt a bit bad about it but the cash is certainly worthwhile to me, even if I have to pay you a slice to keep an eye on me.'

'I'll make it a thin slice,' Craig comforted her. 'It will be a pleasure to keep an eye on you.' He decided he meant it. 'Sounds like money for old rope for both of us.'

'That's what I thought. So much so, that I'm just wondering where the snag comes in.'

Craig told her:

'My department. If there is a snag.'

She said slowly and almost as if she was speaking to herself:

'I did think of going to the police, but it sounds a pretty peculiar story and they would probably say I was wasting their time. I didn't think they would be very understanding.'

'You flatter me,' Craig grinned. 'What

time do you want me to be around?'

She hesitated again then said:

'I think you had better meet me at seven at my — employer's house.' She smiled a little. 'Look, I'll write the address down for you. Can I use this scribbling pad?'

He watched the pencil between her slim fingers travel across the paper. She pushed it over to him and stood up.

'Goodbye.'

He saw her to the door.

'Goodbye, and don't worry. I'll be there at seven.'

*   *   *

At a quarter to seven Craig tapped on the window of his taxi.

'This will do.'

A large moustache craned over its owner's thick shoulder. 'Ain't the address you gave, guv'nor. Only the end of the street. Sure you'll find it if I drops yer 'ere?'

Craig, touched by the driver's solicitude on his behalf, reassured him. He

49

watched the taxi drive off before he turned the corner into a quiet Bloomsbury street.

The Martin girl was waiting for him by the front gate of a small garden halfway down the road.

Craig spoke into the dusk.

'Hallo.'

She pointed up the short path at the end of which the dark mass of the house rose dimly.

'Listen!'

The sound of a piano being played softly and expertly reached their ears. Craig shifted his position a little so that he commanded a better view.

'Set-up couldn't be better,' he said at last. 'It's a good thing it's a warm evening.'

She caught his arm as he started up the path.

'Why?'

'Your boyfriend has the French windows open. I'll stick around. If there's any funny business I'll be through those windows in no time at all.'

'I suppose,' she ventured doubtfully.

'As long as he goes on pounding that piano you will know that I'm all right?'

He grinned at her reassuringly.

'You'll be all right, anyway.'

Her smile was a little tremulous.

'I hope so.'

'Twenty pounds,' he reminded her lightly. 'And I'm here. Go ahead.'

Kay Martin walked firmly up the path and Craig melted into the shrubbery. From the shadows he watched her ring the front door bell. She didn't have to wait long before it was opened by an elderly woman, her hair grey in the glow from the hall light. The next moment Kay was framed in the oblong of light, then the door slammed shut.

Craig lit a cigarette and moved softly nearer the open windows.

'Good evening, Mr. Denby.' Craig could hear her voice, now perfectly steady. 'I have come, you see.'

The old man's voice answered but Craig was too far away to catch the words spoken in a piping reedy tone. There was a short silence in which Craig could imagine the old boy seating himself at the piano, pulling back his cuffs, smoothing his hair in the manner beloved by pianists, and he grinned to himself.

The piano started up again. No doubt about it, he certainly could pound the keyboard. Craig thought the music sounded pretty fine stuff too but, as he had admitted to Kay Martin, he didn't know much about it.

Suddenly the music stopped as abruptly as it had started. It left Craig suspended on top of what he supposed was the climax of the piece.

Cautiously he edged nearer.

The girl was sitting in a corner of the well-furnished room with the house-keeper standing behind her. An enormous grand piano stood at the other end and, as Craig watched, the pale, lined face of Julius Denby, crowned by a magnificent head of thick white hair, peered over the polished lid of the instrument.

'Here, my dear,' the old man was explaining in his piping voice, 'the dramatic movement ends and I come to the quiet passage. Mrs. Horton, perhaps you would tilt the light so that I can see

Miss Martin's face more clearly.'

'Yes, Mr. Denby.'

A gold light slanted across Kay Martin sitting immobile in the big carved chair. Her hands were clenched on her lap and the knuckles showed paper-white through the skin.

Craig thought:

'She's scared stiff.'

At that moment she turned her head towards the window as if to reassure herself of his presence outside. Her expression was calm enough. Craig half wondered if she had seen the glowing tip of his cigarette.

He slid noiselessly back into the shadows.

The music had started again, so peacefully that he had almost been unaware of anyone playing. It was a flowing tranquil passage, played hesitantly at first, and then firmly with growing confidence.

'Ah! Yes!'

Denby's voice had risen with suppressed excitement He was crying out:

'Listen! It's coming to me, now — !
Listen!'

The music grew strong and steady; it filled the room. It spilled into the little garden. Craig thought that to some listening it would have really seemed as if the old man was inspired. As if the girl's loveliness was the impetus urging those hands that plucked at the keyboard.

When the music ceased, there was a long dead silence.

Craig moved forward again. He could see the three people in the room motionless as if caught up in a trance. Kay Martin was the first to move. She stood up stiffly, as though wearied from sitting still so long. Craig could hear the warmth in her modulated voice as she spoke to the old composer.

'That was really marvellous. I — I am so glad if I have been able to help you.'

As her voice trailed off the old man rose shakily to his feet and faced her, supporting himself with one hand on the top of the piano. He was trembling from head to foot but his face was wreathed in smiles.

'I've done it,' he whispered. '*I've done it*. With your help my dear, a great work has been accomplished!'

He seemed almost pathetically happy. Craig, moved as he as he had not been for a long time, lit another cigarette and through the blue smoke watched Julius Denby counting over a wad of notes from his wallet and handing them to Kay Martin. She was about to leave.

Craig moved quickly and worked his way down to the gate.

A few minutes later the front door opened and Kay Martin was moving down the path towards him.

'Well?' he quizzed her humorously as he fell into step beside her. 'Was it worth being inspiring?'

She nodded.

'I feel quite inspired myself. Awe-inspired to think my face brought about *that*!' He didn't answer her.

They had reached the end of the street and Craig was casting a quick eye in the direction of a taxi when she asked seriously:

'How much do I owe you, Mr. Craig?'

He shook his head.

'What do you mean?'

'I couldn't take payment for listening to that music and looking at you. Even if it was in the back row of the pit. Here's your taxi. Where to?'

He slammed the door and repeated the address to the driver before she could start an argument.

★　★　★

About half an hour later he let himself into his flat and clicked on the radio to listen to the news headlines. A smile quirked the corners of his mouth, then he started to laugh. He switched off the radio and left the flat. Grabbing a taxi he rattled back the way he had come.

Outside the house in Bloomsbury he told the driver to wait and walked up the path.

'Mr. Denby is working in the studio,' the grey-haired housekeeper told him in answer to his ring. 'You can hear him.'

Craig looked at her. He said gently: 'I can hear him.'

'He is not to be disturbed.'

The old girl played a good game,

thought Craig, and proceeded to tell her what he was there for. Her tone changed immediately.

'If there's anything — wrong, sir, perhaps you'd tell me.'

Her face was as stony as her voice in the orange light of the hall. He didn't say anything. She went on:

'I've been with Mr. Denby a great number of years, sir — even before his memory became affected.'

Craig began to be interested.

The woman noticed his change of expression.

'He would have been a wonderful composer but for that accident. Years ago, it was, while he was working on a great symphony. He never finished it, because, although he recovered, his creative powers had gone. All he's done since is to remember the music of other composers, honestly believing it is music he himself is writing. I — I do hope you won't disillusion him, sir. He was made so happy tonight because the young lady had, as he thought, inspired him.'

'Take it easy,' he told her. 'I wouldn't

dream of disillusioning him.'

Her features softened into a grateful smile. 'Good night, sir.'

As he walked away, Craig wondered about Kay Martin. If she had known all along and had still taken the twenty quid it was obtaining money under false pretences. Could be. He paused and thoughtfully cupped his hands round his lighter. In the flickering flame he seemed to see her lovely face and he grinned. He'd give her the benefit of the doubt anyway.

After all, he himself wouldn't have known it was some piece by Schubert but for the coincidence of hearing the record and its title when he switched on just before the news headlines.

The Fifth Case:

The Twisted Laugh

It was a few minutes after opening time and the saloon bar of The Bell o'Brixton was pretty empty.

Craig, leaning against the bar and gazing down into his drink, was aware of only one other customer.

He was a tall dark character and Craig didn't fall over himself in admiration for his rather flashy clothes and good looks. The dark character gulped the remainder of his beer, wiping the back of his hand across his mouth and called loudly for plump little Mrs. Donovan to give him the same again.

Craig began to study a playbill on the wall advertising a thriller. This one was being put on next week by the little repertory theatre across the way adjoining a branch of the Southern Bank.

Out of the corner of his eye Craig saw

Mrs. Donovan push another pint over the counter and the dark character had lit a limp cigarette.

'Can I have a word with you?'

The stranger's muttered request only just reached Craig's ear.

Mrs. Donovan's humming ceased abruptly in the middle of a high note. Craig heard her reply amiably:

' 'Course you can.'

'A word,' repeated the other still in the same hoarse whisper, 'alone.'

Craig turned, idly curious, and saw the dark character indicate a door over Mrs. Donovan's shoulder, which was marked: Private.

'What's it all about?'

A suspicious note had crept into Mrs. Donovan's voice.

'Business. Very important business,' muttered the stranger back at her, a slightly sinister emphasis stressing his words.

Mrs. Donovan hesitated.

'Oh, all right. Come into the back room, only I can't give you much time, mind. Bars don't look after themselves.'

The stranger shuffled round the bar and followed Mrs. Donovan into the private sitting room.

Craig suddenly lost interest in the theatrical poster. He slewed quickly round on his heels as the door closed behind the couple, and was left a little ajar.

Craig moved quietly but with the utmost leisure through the bar to the sitting room door.

'Well,' he heard Mrs. Donovan asking the man testily, 'now you're here, what is it you want? I can't waste time with my customers wanting to be served.'

'I'll tell you what I want. I'll tell you, nice and brief. Money.'

'Money?'

Mrs. Donovan sounded incredulous, then became indignant. 'Money, indeed! I'm sorry but I don't lend money to strangers.'

'Who said I was asking you to?'

'But you said — '

'I said,' retorted the stranger, his tone full of meaning, 'I *wanted* money.'

The suspicion had returned to Mrs.

Donovan's voice and with it a tremor of fear. She faltered:

'What do you mean?'

Suddenly the stranger's tone became full of menacing joviality.

'Come now. Be sensible. What I'm doing is, I'm offering to sell you something for your own good.'

'But I don't want to buy anything.'

'You will.'

Through the crack in the door Craig could see him thrust his face viciously forward. He continued:

'You heard of the Brixton Gang?'

Mrs. Donovan nodded dumbly.

'Maybe you remember,' the other went on remorselessly, 'that the Stag had a bit of trouble last week. Smashed up bad it was. The poor old Stag. Fittings, glasses, furnishings. Shocking sight they were by the time the Brixton Gang had finished with 'em.'

Mrs. Donovan found her voice.

'Just what are you getting at?'

The stranger shook his head, ignoring her question.

'Bad business,' he said sadly. 'A very

bad business. And all because they wouldn't listen to reason and buy what I had to offer them.'

He paused, allowing his words to sink in.

He's putting it over quite nicely, Craig thought.

The dark character was at it again: 'Now, you wouldn't like that to happen here, would you?'

'I don't know what you mean.'

' 'Course you know. This little dump of yours is next in the list, see?'

Mrs. Donovan said nothing. The other went on:

'Now, I'm a businessman. I can get your name taken off the list — for a sum.'

Mrs. Donovan gathered her resources.

'You can't threaten me,' she told him indignantly.

The stranger shook his head.

'Stupid,' he sighed. 'Shockingly stupid. In fact, I wouldn't do it if I were you. Much better listen to my little proposition before you do anything as rash as that. We don't want to ruin your business, wreck your pub. It's a nice pub as pubs go,' he added reflectively. 'And neither will happen so long as we get our rake-off. It isn't as if we are asking you for anything you can't afford to pay. Just fifty quid down and a tenner a week from now on.'

A gasp came from Mrs. Donovan.

'You must be raving mad! I haven't got that kind of money — '

'No?'

The other's voice was like ice.

'No,' repeated Mrs. Donovan defiantly. 'I haven't got it, and that's flat.'

The stranger continued suavely as if she hadn't opened her mouth:

'It probably comes as a bit of a shock at first. It usually does. But I'm big-hearted. Always ready to make allowances. Reasonable cove, that's me.'

'You're a dirty crook and if you think you can get away — !'

Mrs. Donovan's voice rose to a crescendo and then Craig became suddenly aware of someone behind him.

He turned swiftly to behold an untidy pink and white man with a cherubic face leaning his elbows on the bar counter and beaming amiably from ear to ear.

Craig raised an eyebrow as the newcomer placed a finger to his lips.

'Sssh!'

The other nodded his head towards the sitting room.

'Some performance, eh?'

Craig agreed it was quite a show.

The pink and white character said pleasantly:

'Don't stop 'em.'

'I wouldn't dream of stopping them,' Craig said. He wanted to hear the end of this act himself.

The stranger's voice came floating out to them. Seemed he was growing impatient.

'You'll save yourself a whole heap of trouble if you play this our way.'

'I tell you I haven't got the money.'

Mrs. Donovan was holding out, but was beginning to hit a somewhat hysterical note.

'Come off it.'

The woman's voice rose, taut with fear.

'Keep your hands off me!'

'Time we interfered,' the pink and white man said in Craig's ear. Craig turned to see he was rocking with silent laughter. 'Not bad. Not bad at all,' he chuckled. He swung round on Craig. 'What do you think of it?'

Craig eyed him levelly.

'Pretty good performer,' he allowed. 'But then Loder always was.'

The other momentarily ceased laughing and frowned at him.

'Loder? His name isn't Loder, it's Warwick. Fenton Warwick. He's an actor after a job. I'm the producer across the way — Guy Fowler's my name — and this is his idea to show me he can act a part in next week's crook play.'

Craig looked at him, then he too started to laugh. When he had recovered sufficiently he said:

'You astonish me.'

'Got you on the hop, did it? Thought it was the real thing, did you? Good! Just how it should be. But I don't think we ought to let the poor woman in there die of fright.'

He brushed past Craig, who was still eyeing him with an amused smile curving his lips.

'All right Mr. Warwick,' called Fowler,

pushing the door open. 'I think you've got the part.'

The dark man released his grip on Mrs. Donovan's wrist as the producer entered the room and turned round, smiling.

'All right, was I?'

'Fine,' Guy Fowler beamed.

The man called Warwick ran a hand over his flashy good looks.

'Hot work,' he exclaimed. 'I think it's back to the bar — and I'll stand a round to celebrate.'

'Look here, what is all this?' Mrs. Donovan had recovered from her fright and was indignantly breathless. 'This man was demanding money! Mr. Fowler, do you *know* him?'

Guy Fowler laughed.

'Yes, I know him. I'm afraid he is just a poor chap after a job, Mrs. Donovan. Come and have a drink with us to make up for the discomfort you've been through.'

'Do you mean to say it was — it was all a game?'

She swung round on the other accusingly.

'I'm awfully sorry, Mrs. Donovan, for

giving you such a bad moment,' Warwick muttered apologetically. 'Do forgive me. But I needed that part in next week's play pretty badly.'

She hesitated a moment then her face relaxed into a smile.

'No one ever accused me of losing my sense of humour and they're not going to now. All the same I'd like that drink, and I don't mind admitting it!'

Fowler and Warwick laughed boisterously and the three of them returned to the bar in the best of spirits.

Craig followed them. He did not appear so amused by it all.

'Hallo, there,' Fowler's voice hailed him. 'Come and join us!'

'Thanks — I will.'

Fowler turned to the other two.

'I found him wondering whether to tackle Warwick single-handed or dial 999,' he chuckled. Then as they all laughed, he asked, still amused: 'Which *would* you have done if I hadn't arrived on the scene of the crime?'

Craig eyed him over the rim of his glass. Then:

'Expect I should have dialled 999,' he said quietly. 'He looked such a realistically tough customer.'

'Convincing, wasn't he?' Fowler agreed and raised his glass.

When the second round was called Craig shook his head.

'Oh, come on,' urged Warwick. He had been looking at him intently.

Craig smiled thinly.

'Got to get along,' he explained. 'Thanks all the same.'

He had started moving towards the door when Warwick made a sudden move after him. 'Here, half a minute,' he said. 'I keep thinking I've seen you before somewhere.'

He wrinkled his brow, puzzling over the problem.

'I don't think so. Just a common type, that's all.'

Under cover of the gusts of laughter, which greeted his reply, Craig eased himself over to the door. But the man called Fowler glanced across at him narrowly as he went out.

Across the road the Southern Bank's

swing doors swung heavily behind Craig's back. He wanted to see the manager, he told the clerk behind the counter.

The manager was a middle-aged capable-looking man who glanced up in surprise as Craig was ushered into his office. By the time Craig had finished talking, he was stunned.

'Good God! I must get on to the police at once.'

Craig smiled without much humour.

'I'll do that, if you like,' he offered.

The manager shook a handkerchief from his pocket and wiped his brow. 'If you would,' he muttered. 'If you would. Very kind.'

He listened to Craig talking incisively into the phone and then, as the receiver was replaced, he asked anxiously:

'All right?'

Craig nodded.

'Nothing to worry about. Scotland Yard are on their way pronto to deal with our friend.'

The other gave a long drawn out exclamation of satisfaction.

'I must say,' he said, 'that was an

extremely ingenious scheme of Loder's. Extremely ingenious. An expert bank-robber like him could, most decidedly, have forced a way in here from the theatre next door. Most decidedly.'

Craig nodded.

'Loder's speciality. Bank-busting is a job he does more easily than another bloke opening a tin of sardines. Afraid he will be slightly disappointed when the police arrive.' He started to laugh as if he had just thought of a good joke.

'My dear fellow! Whatever is so funny about the whole sorry business?'

'I was thinking of that producer. He told me that Loder had me on the hop making me think it was the real thing. I expect he'll be disappointed too at losing such a convincing actor.'

And he laughed again.

The manager was still taking it all very seriously.

'The effrontery of the chap. Putting it over like that and landing the job. If you ask me it was lucky you happened to spot him in the bar and guess who he really was.'

Craig grinned.

'I just added two and two and got the same old number. You see, the Parkville Prison authorities will tell you Loder made quite a hit in the amateur theatricals there. I happened to see him once in the part of a gangster.' Craig rose to his feet, drawing thoughtfully at his cigarette as he observed, 'Got quite a sense of humour, Loder has. In a twisted sort of way, of course.'

The Sixth Case:

The Shady Lady

The man and the girl at the bar in Joe's Place held little interest for Craig. It wasn't always going to be that way, only Craig wasn't to know that. He rated pretty high as a private detective, but he wasn't psychic. There were times when he wished he were. A psychic private eye ought to be able to come up with any of the answers at any time. On the other hand, maybe it was just as well not to know too much about the future, but just take it as it came.

He glanced idly at the man who was Larry Dell — a small-time crook operating in devious ways round the greyhound tracks. The girl Craig didn't know. Some shady lady he surmised Larry had managed to attract in his repulsive way. She was pretty, if you liked them hard and glittering and tough. He had to admit that anyone who went around with Larry needed to be tough, at that. Larry Dell wasn't at all the subtle type.

As he turned to his drink, from the corner of his eye Craig noticed Larry pass a letter over to the girl. She read it intently. Then there was a short, tense discussion between her and the man, but Craig couldn't hear what they said. The radio was blaring too loudly. Craig didn't think he could ask Joe to turn it down, so that he could overhear someone else's conversation. Even in that dive, it wouldn't be quite the thing.

The girl won her argument with Larry, anyhow, and pushed the letter into her handbag. It was then Craig asked himself what there was in it for him and turned his interest to his evening paper.

He didn't notice Larry and the girl go out. A little later, when he said good night to Joe, the place was empty except for a scruffy-looking individual who seemed to be half-asleep in a corner.

'Good night, Mr. Craig,' Joe called out and grinned. 'Wake up Dusty for me as

74

you go, before he starts snoring!'

Craig glanced at the man in the corner as he passed and at that moment there was a sound as if a car had backfired in the street. The scruffy-looking character woke up with a start, glared at Craig blearily and muttered himself off into a doze again.

Craig went on up the dark stairs and reached the dingy passage that led to the street. He paused to light a cigarette and then, suddenly, his gaze shifted to the door of the phone booth a few feet along the passage. The door of the booth was open and the dim light inside showed a dark figure crumpled in a heap.

Craig pulled the door wide, bent, and after a moment or two straightened himself. So it hadn't been a car back-firing after all. He stood for a moment staring down at the inert shape at his feet, then turned and went back down the stairs to the bar.

The scruffy-looking individual was still dreaming in the corner, his mouth half-open, his head lolled to one side. As Craig went in, Joe looked up from the sports page with surprise.

'Back so soon, Mr. Craig? You ain't been long.'

'Who was the dark girl who just went out?'

Joe gave him a puzzled frown before he said:

'You mean the one with Larry?'

Craig nodded. He said:

'I mean the one with Larry.'

'Ruby Scott,' Joe said. 'Dance hostess at the Stardrome.' He jerked a thumb in the direction which Craig took as indicating the locale of a nearby dance-hall. Then he leered at him: 'Why — if it isn't a rude answer?'

Craig eyed him bleakly.

'Curiosity, that's all,' he said. 'By the way,' he added casually over his shoulder, 'I think you should call the police. There's a body in your phone box.'

Joe goggled at him.

'You — you mean Ruby?'

Craig shook his head.

'Larry Dell,' he said.

Craig turned on his heel and passed the scruffy-looking character in the corner

76

who suddenly toppled over and fell flat on his face. He woke up and let fly a stream of highly coloured abuse as Craig went on up the stairs towards the street.

A taxi put him down outside the large building with 'Stardrome' glittering from it in neon lights. The dancehall occupied a prominent site on a corner at the back of Oxford Street. Its career had been varied and it had passed through many hands before it had been taken over by a syndicate and had blossomed forth as a super dancehall, with a couple of large and noisy dance bands taking turns to keep the music going for their patrons.

Craig went in to the crowded ballroom where the dance band blared out a treacly tune and coloured spotlights played on the sardine-packed dancers.

There were several faces he recognized. He didn't care for any of them particularly. Cheap crooks, they were, some of them a bunch of the Riverside Boys, plus their girls. Sleek, with their shoulders over-padded, and wary-eyed.

Then Craig spotted the one he wanted and, stubbing out his cigarette, pushed

77

his way round the dance floor.

'Hallo, Ruby ... may 1 have the pleasure?'

Ruby Scott slanted him a cold stare from beneath her heavily mascaraed eyelashes. After a moment she said:

'If you've got the money, I suppose you've got the right to use my shoes to walk around on.'

He grinned at her.

'That's what I guessed would be the big attraction about you,' he said. 'Your charm.'

She didn't bother to answer him. Deliberately she took a mirror from her handbag slung on the chair beside her. She gave herself plenty of time, dolling up her face, before she replaced the hand-mirror. Then, condescendingly, she moved into his arms. They danced silently for a while before she admitted grudgingly:

'You know where to put your feet.'

'You keep in step yourself,' he told her.

She looked up at him with veiled curiosity.

'Who told you my name?'

'I get around.' Then he said, casually: 'Friend of Larry Dell, aren't you?' He felt her stiffen in his arms. 'What's the matter?'

Now her gaze was wide with suspicion. She said:

'You were in Joe's dump just now.'

He nodded.

They danced some more without a word until she said:

'Thought I'd seen you somewhere. What you after?'

'What should I be after?'

She didn't answer. Just stared at him unblinkingly.

As they passed the spot where they'd started to dance, the lights dimmed suddenly. Then a purple spotlight bobbed over the dancers, giving their faces strangely contorted expressions. Then all the lights were up again and the music stopped.

'I'm sitting out the next dance,' Ruby said hurriedly, almost nervously.

'Too bad — ' he started to say and then broke off as two girls pushed past. One, a plump redhead, was speaking animatedly:

'Hope Wally Gold isn't all booked up — he's my favourite — !'

Craig turned from Ruby Scott and watched the girls hurry up to a group of bored, sleek-looking young men. Idly he watched the plump redhead practically throw herself into the arms of one of them. After a moment he turned back to Ruby, gave her an enigmatic smile and walked away.

He felt her chill, speculative stare in the back of his neck as he left her.

The music was starting up again as he went out of the ballroom and into the street. He paused in the cool air and thoughtfully lit a cigarette. A taxi pulled up and a man and girl got out and hurried into the dancehall. As the driver pushed up his flag again, Craig told him to take him back to Joe's Place.

When he arrived, he found the late and unlamented Larry Dell had been removed, but the fingerprints men were busy working over the phone box. Craig went on downstairs and found Inspector Ward talking to Joe. The Inspector turned to him as he came in and said, with heavy humour:

'Nice of you, Craig, to come back and explain why you breezed off into the night after you found Larry Dell. Or maybe,' he went on sourly, 'you're going to tell me you've got the person who did him in?'

'Quite the mind-reader, aren't you?' Craig said.

He flipped something on to the bar counter. The Inspector picked it up, his eyes narrow.

He growled:

'Where'd you find this?'

Craig didn't answer while the other concentrated on the letter in his hand. Then the Inspector said:

'Get around, don't you?'

Craig eyed him with bleak amusement.

'Funny you should mention that,' he said. 'I was telling someone else the same thing just now.'

'Where?'

Craig grinned at him.

'Ever go dancing, Inspector?'

★   ★   ★

81

The police car pulled up with a jerk outside the Stardrome and Inspector Ward got out, followed by Craig. The Inspector turned to the driver and told him to hang around. Then, as they moved towards the dancehall entrance, he grunted to Craig:

'I've known this dump since it was an auction-room. Used to have roller-skating here, too, I remember.'

As they paused inside the foyer of the Stardrome, a uniformed attendant came forward to meet them with a polite inquiry. Inspector Ward informed him he had an appointment with the manager. The man directed them to an office at the top of a heavily carpeted flight of stairs and they went in.

Craig sat back and listened while the manager answered the Scotland Yard man's questions and then picked up the internal phone and gave an instruction. Craig figured he'd done his share, and it wasn't his case anyway. It was just one of those things he'd happened to stumble on and he'd lent a helping hand. He reminded himself to remember to mention it to

Ward one of these days when *he* wanted some cooperation from the Inspector.

The door opened and a dark, sleek-looking individual came in.

Inspector Ward started throwing leading questions at the newcomer.

The answers came guardedly and with reluctance.

'You say you never heard of this Larry Dell?' Inspector Ward rasped.

'Not until you mentioned him,' was the surly reply.

Ward went on with grim patience. He asked:

'What about Ruby Scott?'

'I know her casually,' the other admitted. 'Working here together, we are bound to meet and speak to each other — naturally.'

'Naturally . . . '

There was a little pause. Wally Gold's eyes flickered from Inspector Ward to Craig and the manager, and back to the Inspector again. Ward was taking something out of his pocket to slap it down on the table between them. He drew a deep breath and said, deliberately:

'Seeing that you never knew Larry Dell and are only casually acquainted with Ruby Scott, perhaps you'd explain *that?*'

Wally Gold's jaw sagged. Ward threw Craig a triumphant glance, then turned on the other and grunted:

'I'll read it to you, if you like . . . One of the things we dumb cops have learnt to do is to read!'

Wally Gold still couldn't think up a thing to say. He just watched with glazed eyes while the Inspector unfolded the letter he'd banged down on the table.

'It's addressed to Larry Dell,' he said. Then he read, slowly:

'This is to warn you: keep off the grass. Ruby is my girl so don't try and take her away from me or I'll take care of you. I'm not being funny.'

★　★　★

Inspector Ward paused to glance over the letter at the dark man who wasn't looking so sleek now. He queried:

'And do you know who it's signed by? Wally Gold!'

After Wally Gold had been taken away, Inspector Ward and Craig stood in the foyer of the dancehall, the dance orchestra still churning out the treacly music behind them. The Inspector was asking curiously:

'Wonder which one the girl is, or was, in love with? Dell, or Wally Gold?'

Craig contemplated the tip of his cigarette for a moment.

'Maybe it was Wally,' he said. 'That was why she took care of his letter to Larry when he showed it to her in the bar. Then, when Larry was bumped off a little later while waiting for her, she guessed Wally had done it and her love changed to sudden hatred — she's the type who switch around like that. She was too scared to squeak to the police, but she was going to see Wally get his, all right.'

Inspector Ward was tapping a foot to the rhythm of the music. He nodded slowly and observed sententiously:

'Women are funny that way.' He thought it over for a moment, then turned to Craig with a look of reluctant admiration. 'Pretty smart of you,' he said, 'getting that letter of Wally's off her. How did you — while you were dancing?'

'Who said I got it off her?' Craig wanted to know. The other's heavy eyebrows were lifted in inquiry. He asked:

'Where did you get it?'

Craig smiled at him through a cloud of cigarette smoke.

'I was starting to tell you,' he said. 'She'd made up her mind Wally wasn't going to get away with it. I got that letter off Larry Dell himself.' The Inspector was frowning at him. He hadn't caught on. 'Don't you get it?' Craig continued. 'Ruby had planted it there — deliberately.'

The Seventh Case:

The Strange Business in Bond Street

The phone jangled on Craig's desk and he eyed the instrument with marked disfavour.

The ringing rasped his nerves, exasperated his patience, played hell with his longing to relax. Why couldn't some people understand that even London's most successful private detective had moments of hankering to get away from it all and escape the hurly-burly of the metropolis remote for a remote South Sea Island with shelving beaches and surfboards and maybe a Hula-Hula girl or two thrown in.

The ringing persisted.

Craig reached across a weary hand, keeping his feet on the desk, and admitted his identity without enthusiasm.

'This is Colonel Taverton!'

Craig winced as the voice in his ear

blasted the last fragile fragment of his palm-tree dream into fine dust.

'Yes?'

Craig sounded as if he couldn't be less interested.

'I'm speaking from Ramon's, the hairdresser's in Bond Street.'

'Do you usually go to Ramon's?' Craig asked Colonel Taverton pleasantly but with a decidedly disinterested emphasis. Unfortunately the Colonel was far too concerned with his own private grief to be choked off.

His voice grated in Craig's ear.

'My daughter's just been robbed. Can you get round here as soon as possible.' The request was clearly an order.

Craig made one last effort.

'Won't the police do as well?'

'No, no!'

Colonel Taverton was getting more and more hot under the collar and Craig knew precisely what he would like. He groaned inwardly.

'My daughter,' spat the Colonel, 'abhors publicity. The idea of being mixed up in police proceedings — '

He broke off as if the prospect was too horrible to contemplate. 'All she wants is her sapphire necklace back.'

'That's fine.'

'It's a family heirloom. All she wants,' repeated the Colonel, 'is its return. Without worrying about the thief.'

'H'm,' said Craig thoughtfully.

'What?'

'I was thinking it would be quite a trick getting stolen goods back and not bothering over the chap who pinched 'em. My fees would be much higher.'

But he was wasting his time on the Colonel whose sense of humour could be placed on a pinhead without being crowded for space. Colonel Taverton said:

'Ask what you like, it makes no difference to me. *I want that necklace back!*'

Craig perceived he was chatting with a one-track mind.

'All right. I'll be over.'

'Good,' the Colonel approved. 'And hurry.'

'I'll grab a taxi,' Craig promised without bothering to stifle a yawn. The

Colonel hung up.

When Craig arrived, he padded over Ramon's thickly carpeted floor to Ramon's luxurious private office and there in the doorway was Ramon himself looking anxiety itself from his shiny shoes to his pencil moustache.

'A-aah,' he bleated when he saw Craig. 'Mr. Craig? My poor client! Unfortunate, oh, so unfortunate — '

'Mr. Craig?'

Colonel Taverton stopped pacing the floor space and came forward. He looked even more like his voice than Craig had imagined.

There was a short pause while Colonel and Miss Taverton registered their surprise all over their faces and Craig's sardonic smile broadened. He knew what they had expected; someone in outsize boots, bowler hat and one eye a permanent wink through putting the other to keyholes in divorce cases.

Craig acknowledged his identity uncompromisingly. This girl was an attractive piece and knew it. She was sitting in a low armchair furnished with white cushions and obviously reserved for Ramon's exclusive clientele. After she had got over her initial surprise at Craig's appearance she promptly turned all her charm on him.

'I'm so glad you have come,' she cried. 'It's all so terrible, this sort of thing happens to other people but somehow one never expects it to happen to oneself.'

She opened wide her blue eyes and contrived to look helpless. Craig took a drag at his cigarette and waited for her to stop talking.

'Mr. Craig,' she went on, working harder on the appealing note, 'Mr. Craig, you do think you'll be able to get my necklace back for me. Don't you?'

He answered her cheerfully:

'Haven't the slightest idea.'

'Dammit — !' exploded Colonel Taverton. 'Isn't that what you're here for?'

Craig smiled sweetly at him.

'Maybe your daughter would tell me what happened.'

'But of course I will.' Miss Taverton pressed her fingers to her forehead.

Watching her, Craig was reminded of a

girl he had known long ago and far away. A girl who had spent *her* life at dressmakers, beauty parlours, hairdressers and jewellers, as obviously did Miss Taverton

'Yes,' she was saying. 'I collected the necklace from Vincent's — '

'The jewellers,' put in her father.

'They had been repairing it — '

'Clasp gone,' explained Colonel Taverton.

'It was such a beautiful thing,' went on his daughter. 'I didn't want to lose it, and now — '

'Antique sapphire necklace,' obliged Colonel Taverton. 'Sort of family heirloom. Gave it to Myra on her twenty-first birthday.'

Myra smiled at him affectionately

'Apart from what it's worth,' she said to Craig, 'it has great sentimental value for me — '

The Colonel cut in again. 'Of course it has.'

Craig asked:

'And what happened after you left Vincent's?'

'I came straight here for my hair

appointment,' replied Myra promptly. 'The necklace was in its case, wrapped up, and I slipped it into my coat pocket which I left on the chair.'

Craig raised his brows.

'Rather careless?'

She glanced down at her expensive handbag lying on Ramon's polished desk.

'I realize that now,' she nodded. Her eyes flew to Craig's face again as if imploring him to understand. 'But one is apt not to — to think of things like robberies. Well, anyway, after I had had my shampoo and my hair had been set the girl put me under the drier and left me. I started reading a magazine.'

She paused.

'And?' prompted Craig.

'The cubicle I was in,' she continued, 'was nearest the entrance. I heard the street door open and I thought it was Daddy coming to fetch me for lunch. The next thing I knew somebody was slipping in very quietly and I looked up just in time to see a man take the necklace out of my pocket. Naturally I screamed.'

Craig looked at her.

'Naturally.'

She eyed him suspiciously.

'Oh, I know you are used to these things. But I was terrified. He dashed out and of course, by the time I was able to get myself out from beneath the drier, he had gone.'

Craig regarded her sympathetically.

'They are the darndest things.'

'What are?' It was the irate Colonel Taverton who barked at him.

'Driers.'

Craig smiled at him innocently.

Myra, finding the attention that she felt was rightfully hers was slipping from her, moaned:

'Oh, it was terrible. Terrible!'

Colonel Taverton picked up his cue dutifully and patted her shoulder while Ramon made clucking noises of distress.

Craig felt it was about time he started to earn his fee. He had one or two points he wanted cleared up. He queried:

'The necklace is insured, of course?'

The Colonel nodded. Craig turned to the girl.

'Can you describe the man?'

94

She sensed the change in his attitude. She stared at him for a moment, then she said thoughtfully:

'He was youngish, thin-faced, wore a raincoat and light grey hat.'

'A nice precise answer,' Craig congratulated her but before she could reply the Colonel interrupted.

'I arrived just after it happened. My daughter was in a most awful state, as you can imagine.'

Craig said, 'I can imagine.'

'My theory is,' the Colonel rambled on, 'the thief followed her from the jewellers and — '

Craig let him ramble. He turned to the girl.

'Anything else you can remember that might help?'

She corrugated her smooth brow. 'No, I can't remember anything else — ' she broke off suddenly and exclaimed: 'Yes there was. The telephone.' She rounded on Ramon. 'Just before the man came in I heard you answer the telephone at the desk. You said something about you'd go and see, and I heard you hurry along to

95

one of the cubicles.'

'Ah — !'

Ramon thought painfully, recollection broke upon him and he nodded violently.

'Miss Taverton is perfectly correct.' He bowed to Myra. 'The girl who should have been at the desk was out having coffee. I took her place. We are — like everywhere — so short-staffed.'

He shrugged his shoulders apologetically.

'The phone call?' Craig said gently. It seemed to be his job this morning to thread conversations together.

'It was a man wanting to speak with one of the assistants,' Ramon explained abruptly. 'I do not encourage personal calls among the staff. However, he seemed insistent and said it was important so I told him to hold on while I went and found her. She was very busy and had no idea who it could be so I came back to ask if he would leave a message with me and found Miss Taverton crying out her necklace had been stolen. I picked up the phone, but the caller had rung off.'

He drew his brows together in a thoughtful frown. He said slowly:

'I did not think about it at the time, I was so distressed with this business. But now, when I do think, it is peculiar he rang off when he was so insistent before.'

Craig asked him:

'What time was that?'

'About . . . yes, about eleven-thirty.'

'Did you see this man diving into the street?'

Ramon shook his head.

'I'd like to have a word with the girl who did Miss Taverton's hair,' Craig said.

Ramon said:

'That is Lily. I will fetch her for you immediately.'

'Save it,' Craig told him. 'I'll find her.'

Lily — small, brunette and scared — was clearing up in the same cubicle where she had attended Miss Taverton.

Craig smiled at her genially and she obligingly corroborated the Taverton girl's story.

Through a spiral of cigarette smoke, Craig eyed her dispassionately. She was a somewhat nervous type, he decided.

'So you left Miss Taverton under the drier? Where did you go then?'

'I — I just went along to help one of the other girls with a perm,' Lily told him unhappily. She wasn't exactly at ease answering his questions.

He nodded and put her out of her agony.

'I think that's all.'

He went back to the office with a smile etching his features but he was a trifle unprepared for what happened. The sound of a rush and flurry behind him and Ramon staring rigidly over his shoulder all seemed to occur at one and the same time.

Ramon yelled:

'Lily, *Lily*, where are you going?' With excited cries Ramon brushed Craig aside, shouting, 'Lily! Stop — where are you off to — ?'

Craig regarded him mildly for a second then he turned back into the office and grinned engagingly at Colonel Taverton and his daughter. Myra was on her feet and both she and her father seemed rooted to the spot.

Craig said chattily:

'Poor old Ramon will have to make it snappy. Lily is a pretty fast mover.'

Myra threw a startled glance at the crumpled white coat lying on the floor just outside the office where Lily had dropped it *en route* for the street.

'The thief's accomplice!' she exclaimed. 'That's who she is. She realized you had found her out, and now she's escaping. Mr. Craig, why don't you *do* something?'

He eyed her silently. Then he drew a deep breath.

'I'm disappointed in you, Miss Taverton,' he said.

'What — what do you mean?'

Colonel Taverton barked irritably:

'What are you standing there for, telling my daughter you're disappointed in her when that girl is getting away?' He made a grab at Craig's arm. 'Confound it, that woman knows where the necklace is. If you're a detective at all, get along after her!'

Gently Craig disengaged himself.

'I am a detective, Colonel Taverton. Unfortunately,' he added urbanely, 'I'm rather a good one.'

The Colonel looked at him pop-eyed.

'Unfortunately?'

Craig dragged at his cigarette and flicked some ash on Ramon's beautiful carpet before he nodded. His eyes roved the room and came to rest on Myra Taverton.

He said engagingly:

'Unfortunately for Miss Taverton.'

The Colonel gaped at him incredulously.

'My daughter?'

Myra was blinking at Craig as if he were something out of this world.

'I don't know what you're talking about,' she choked. 'That girl.' She flung out her hand dramatically, pointing to the swinging entrance door Ramon had left open. 'That girl — !'

Craig cut in.

'Never mind her. The poor kid got a bit scared being questioned and panicked — that's all.'

Colonel Taverton's face grew more lobster-like. He tried to recover some poise, while he repeated his old blustering formula:

'What the devil d'you mean, 'Unfortunately for my daughter'?'

'I mean,' Craig told him placidly, 'that it is unfortunate for her she made all this fuss in the first place. Since she knows where the necklace is.'

There was a second's shocked silence.

Craig's remark seemed to dance around the Colonel's bemused head, punching all the bluster out of him. His jaw dropped. He said nothing, but sagged forward at Craig in a mute appeal for a further explanation.

Craig murmured dispassionately:

'That fairytale she dreamed up about hearing the door open, the phone going and the thief creeping in. You know really she couldn't possibly have heard any of it. Her pretty, stupid head was under the drier at the time.'

'Myra — ?'

It was barely a croak the Colonel threw at his daughter as he swung round on her. He didn't have to ask more, the truth was written over every inch of her frightened face.

Promptly, automatically almost, she

burst into floods of tears. Her performance left Craig cold, it was so phoney. But it sent her father into a rage that looked as though it might turn into an apoplectic fit.

'I didn't mean any harm, Daddy,' she wailed. 'Only I owe a lot of money and — and I had to pay my debts somehow, so I sold the necklace.'

'Sold the — !'

Colonel Taverton was, for once, bereft of speech.

'I knew you'd be furious. That's why I thought I'd pretend it had been stolen, and I got a — a friend of mine to ring up to make it sound more convincing. It wasn't going to hurt anybody — '

'Except,' cut in Craig coldly, 'Lily. You were quite willing she should be suspected.'

'I was frightened.'

Colonel Taverton turned to Craig.

'I don't know what to say. I can only offer my apologies and, naturally, you will be paid just the same.'

Craig began to feel a twinge of pity for the old man, then he thought of his wasted morning.

'By the way,' Colonel Taverton asked Craig as he re-capped his fountain pen, 'how do you come to know so much about women's hairdressers?'

Craig's smile was a trifle wry.

'Used to know a girl rather like your daughter. She ran around a lot too. Only chance I ever had to get her to myself was at the hairdressers. It was having to shout I loved her with that drying thing over her head that finally bust our romance.'

The Eighth Case:

The Christmas Eve Ghost

Sophie Forrest was blue-eyed and pretty, like a china doll, and her face was about as hard. Craig let his gaze run down to her very shapely legs advantageously displayed in sheerest stockings.

She didn't look the type to scare easily and yet here she was leaning across his desk, saying:

'I'm scared and I'm admitting it. I just didn't know who to turn to for help, then I thought of you.'

Craig was accustomed to this angle but it never ceased to flatter him slightly.

'Have a cigarette,' he offered. 'Now,' he added as they lit up. 'You don't really believe in this spook do you?'

'Seeing is believing, isn't it? I've seen it all right — two nights running.'

'The ghost of a Burmese dancing girl,' murmured Craig thoughtfully to himself.

He was beginning to be interested, especially as he hadn't expected anything out of the ordinary to come his way on Christmas Eve. He had resigned himself to a series of phone calls asking him to go and guard the family silver at Christmas house-parties.

Sophie Forrest pulled raggedly at her cigarette and managed to smile.

'I know it sounds quite ridiculous to you, Mr. Craig,' she said in the voice of one who didn't see anything ridiculous in it at all, 'but it does tie up with the old story.'

Craig told her:

'Better get the whole thing off your chest. Up to date all I know is that the house is supposed to be haunted by a Burmese dancer and you've seen her. What more?'

She flicked a golden flake of tobacco off her lip with a red-tipped finger before she answered him.

'Years ago it seems, the house was owned by some Eastern prince who kept this dancing girl there and then eventually killed her in a fit of jealous rage. The general idea now, is that she appears every year at Christmas time.'

'And how long have you been in the house, Mrs. Forrest?'

She smiled wryly.

'This is my first Christmas — and my last, I'm beginning to think! When my husband and I took the house last summer to convert into an hotel we merely thought it was silly nonsense.'

Craig asked:

'And your husband? Has he seen it? What does he think now?'

She hesitated. When she spoke it was slowly and she kept her eyes on the tip of her cigarette. She said:

'Nick — my husband — is dead.'

Craig's brows contracted.

'Was it a sudden death, Mrs. Forrest?'

She nodded.

'He was found in the river early one morning two months ago. He'd been shot.'

'Naturally, you had the police in.'

This was definitely more in his line than the unhappy spirits of Burmese dancing girls.

106

'They can't find out who did it. I don't believe they ever will.'

Craig was remembering newspaper reports of some young Putney hotel proprietor being pulled out of the river. At the time it had sounded to him like a murder job. He said only:

'So you're running the place alone now?'

She shook her head.

'No. My husband's partner is still there. Mr. Craig — '

But he interrupted to ask:

'Has he been scared by the ghost too?'

'He saw it before I did. The next night we waited up together to see if it came again. It did.'

'Exactly what sort of a performance does this dancing girl put over?'

'Scoff if you like, Mr. Craig. It isn't so funny once you've seen it. She suddenly appears in the corridor — from nowhere, it seemed to me, but Arthur said he thought she walked right through the wall — then she cries out: 'I'll haunt this house' twice and the second time she adds: 'Until my death be avenged!' It's always the same words. Then she disappears.'

Craig remained unimpressed.

'Looks like somebody will have to avenge her death then,' he remarked lightly. 'If she is indeed a ghost. What does she look like?'

Sophie Forrest shuddered.

'Horrible. Wild, with blood all over her dress and black hair falling about her face.'

He regarded her silently for a moment. Then:

'What do you want me to do about it?'

'I thought,' and there was a touch of pleading in her voice, 'that if you would come down tonight and see for yourself, as an outsider you know, it would help. Then, if it is a ghost, I suppose I shall have to get out. It's scared off everybody in the hotel so there won't be much point in staying anyway.'

'How are you going to pass me off? As a ghost-layer, a guest or just myself?'

She answered him quickly.

'A guest. Pretend you have come to stay over Christmas.'

'What is your partner's name besides Arthur?'

'Lennox. Arthur Lennox. He says he is going to shoot at the thing if it shows up again tonight.'

'Which, if it is a spook,' Craig observed, 'won't inconvenience it much. All right, I'll come. It's one way of spending Christmas Eve that I haven't tried yet.'

She didn't answer him but stood up, collecting her bag and gloves off the desk.

'I'll be along in time for dinner,' said Craig. 'I hope your plum pudding's good.'

'It's good,' she said.

He wondered if she really hadn't any sense of humour or whether it had all been knocked out of her by the goings-on at Putney.

He saw her politely to the door.

'By the by,' he said, 'you haven't told anybody about me?'

'Nobody.'

'Not even Lennox?'

She stared at him.

'I said nobody, Mr. Craig.'

He leant against the doorpost, whistling

softly to himself as she disappeared down the stairs; then, the whistle still on his lips, he went quickly back to his desk. He sat down and put his feet up in their favourite position. He might as well be comfortable; he had a number of telephone calls to make.

When he hung up finally from his chats with the Putney police and Scotland Yard, he leant thoughtfully back in his chair and gazed intently at the ceiling.

Among other items that interested him quite a lot, he had learned that the late Mr. Nick Forrest had a brother.

★ ★ ★

River View Private Hotel stood dark and dismal in its own grounds, the mist from the river swirling about its gaunt grimness.

'Blimey!' exclaimed the dejected-looking little individual who had clambered out of the taxi at Craig's heels. 'Looks okay for all the works and no mistake.'

'Setting certainly has atmosphere,' Craig agreed.

He turned away from the illuminated meter of the taxi and stood looking up the drive. He laughed light-heartedly.

'Never mind. Mrs. Forrest should have a nice comforting drink ready and waiting.'

'Couldn't be any readier than I am,' the other retorted.

Their footsteps crunched up the drive, Craig's companion trotting miserably in the rear, muttering:

'Christmas Eve too. Cor!'

The door was flung open as soon as they set foot on the steps, and Craig had a shrewd suspicion their approach had been watched by Sophie Forrest from some unlighted window.

'Mr. Craig,' she said swiftly, glancing back for a moment over her shoulder. 'Come in. Your room is all ready for you.'

Her welcoming manner couldn't disguise her nervousness. She caught sight of the other man as he followed Craig into the lighted hall.

'Who is he?'

Craig said easily:

'This is Brown. He wishes to spend

111

Christmas here for want of a better place to go. His wife has just left him.' Craig encountered a startled look from the woman. He grinned at her. 'I shall want another room,' he said firmly.

His voice was loud enough to benefit any inquisitive ears that might be listening.

Later in the evening Craig found Arthur Lennox was the jovial and hearty type. When dinner was over Arthur became the life and soul of the party. Despite the fact that there wasn't anybody in the place with the exception of the three men, Mrs. Forrest and a pudding-faced stolid maid, he was full of a misguided Christmas spirit plus jokes which sounded as if they had come out of a cracker and were about as funny. Unlike Sophie Forrest, who was very silent, the possible appearance of any ghostly visitation did not seem to worry him.

At ten thirty Craig could take it no longer.

'If you will excuse me, Mrs. Forrest, I think I will go to bed.' He included the man he'd called Brown with a movement of his head. 'It's been a somewhat exhausting day.'

'It's early,' Arthur Lennox protested.

'Mr. Brown always goes to bed early,' said Craig piously.

The big clock down in the darkened hall had struck half past eleven when there was a light tap on Craig's door. He opened it without switching on the light.

It was Sophie Forrest.

'I just wanted to make sure you were ready,' she whispered.

He answered in a low voice:

'I'll be there when the fun starts.'

She nodded, satisfied, and crept silently away. At a few minutes to midnight Craig's door slowly opened again.

'We'll get in the shadow of that doorway,' Craig told Brown quietly. The other, who was peering over his shoulder, nodded. Noiselessly they approached the shadows Craig had indicated. Craig glanced at his watch. The luminous dial showed twelve o'clock. Almost at once a gentle scraping noise broke the quiet of the house and something seemed to emerge from the wall a few yards away.

"Strewth,' whispered Craig's companion inelegantly. 'The ruddy ghost!'

'But *not,*' murmured Craig, 'of the Burmese dancing girl.'

As he spoke Craig became aware of Sophie Forrest and Arthur Lennox waiting in the darkness farther down the passage. The apparition was making straight for them.

A sudden gasp from Sophie shattered the tension.

'Nick! It's Nick!'

'It can't be!'

It was Lennox who cried out, but he shrank farther back as the terrifying figure, looking as if it had climbed out of the river, slowly advanced, stabbing an accusing finger.

Lennox flung out a hand as if to ward it off.

'Go away!' he shrieked. 'Go away! Don't touch me!'

The figure laughed hollowly, and in deep, sepulchral tones said:

'You know who I am, Arthur Lennox. I am Nick Forrest.'

Lennox was gibbering.

114

'Don't look at me like that — Go away — *go away*!'

'Nick Forrest,' repeated the advancing figure relentlessly. 'Accusing my murderer!'

Lennox was wild-eyed.

'I didn't mean it, Nick, I didn't mean to kill you. Don't come any nearer!' His voice rose to a scream.

The man beside Craig drew a long whistle and Sophie Forrest, crouched against the wall, forgot her terror for a second:

'So it *was* you who did it!'

At the sound of her words something seemed to snap in Lennox's benumbed brain. He pushed her aside and a gun gleamed in his hand.

'Keep away!' he yelled at the approaching figure. 'Stand away, I tell you!'

The answer he got was another hollow cackle.

Then a report roared through the house. Another and another as Lennox fired at pointblank range. There was a moment of silence as Lennox realized that the apparition was still moving towards him. The gun clattered from his grasp. He gave a strangled noise in his throat and slid to the floor in a dead faint.

'Very nice,' observed Craig coolly as the girl turned and fled down the stairs. Craig and Brown emerged from the doorway.

'All right, Bill.'

At Craig's voice the apparition turned and remarked cheerfully:

'Not so bad, eh? Looks like we proved the blighter did kill poor old Nick.'

'Never said a truer word.' It was the man called Brown speaking in a tone of deep satisfaction as he snapped a pair of handcuffs over Lennox's wrists. He straightened up. 'And I don't mind admitting as you gave *me* a bit of a turn once or twice.'

Craig chuckled and went downstairs in search of Sophie Forrest.

He found her huddled in a corner of the sofa in the lounge.

'What you need,' he told her, 'is a good stiff drink. Where do I find you one? And one for my friends?' When he returned she said:

'Please explain. I feel a little weak.'

Handing her a glass and grinning, he told her:

'Get outside this first.'

She took it gratefully and Craig sat down beside her. 'Sorry I had to scare you that way,' he apologized. 'But I wasn't sure if you were in on your husband's murder or not.'

She smiled at him wanly over the rim of her glass.

'I had a feeling all along it was Arthur Lennox who killed him but there didn't seem to be any proof.'

Craig told her:

'The Putney police had the same feeling too. His aim, of course, was to scare you off, which would have left him with the hotel all to himself. Pretty crude stuff,' he reflected, 'but he might have got away with it.'

She gulped her drink.

'Do you think he's mad?'

'Most people think murderers are mad. It was such an elaborate set-up I would say Lennox may have had some sort of a kink.'

She asked:

'You guessed the ghost was phoney from the start, didn't you?'

He nodded.

'When you gave me her little speech,' he said, 'it didn't sound so very much like Burmese to me.'

She began to laugh shakily.

'Why, of course. She wouldn't have spoken in English!'

He grinned at her.

'Exactly. One of his girlfriends popping through the secret panel he'd discovered. I knew there must be one if the apparition was flesh and blood, and it was pretty easy to find after you had pointed the spot out to me where it always did its disappearing act. I found the girl friend there this evening and your husband's brother just took her place. Didn't you know about him?'

She shook her head.

'I knew of him but I had never met him.'

'He is an actor out of a job, so — I gave him a job.'

She looked incredulous.

'And he took it, knowing he risked being shot?'

Craig smiled quietly.

'You told me Lennox was going to take a pot-shot at his dancing-girl,' he said, 'so I knew he'd be demonstrating with blanks to give the right ghostly effect.'

He raised his glass and said:

'Happy Christmas!'

The Ninth Case:

Jewels Into Thin Air

The smell of fresh paint hung sickeningly on the air as Craig sauntered up the semi-circular drive of Mrs. Clarence Osborne's house in Regent's Park.

As he rounded the shrubbery, numerous signboards advertising the name of a well-known firm in large letters hit him in the eye. There were long ladders propped against the walls. A heavy decorating job was underway.

Craig went up the shallow steps two at a time and a cadaverous-faced butler opened the door in answer to his summons on the bell.

'This way, if you please, sir,' he murmured in the hushed accents of one about to enter a morgue.

As they moved through the hall Craig cocked an eyebrow at the amazing sight that welcomed him.

On one side, six characters in white overalls were sheepishly regarding their toes as they ranged the wall. Facing them, in front of a massive hallstand, three women servants were lined up. They didn't look as if they were having much fun either.

Craig found himself in the library with the door closing softly behind him and wondered vaguely whether the dignified butler had gone to join the guard of honour in the hall.

His musings were interrupted by the owner of the same hysterical tones that had quavered at him over the phone earlier in the day.

Mrs. Clarence O. was fat and definitely well over forty. She may have been a blonde in her own right years ago, Craig decided unkindly, but the gold hair, which glinted at him now was by right of her hairdresser. She was crowded into a highly expensive silk dress, which had ceased to look expensive. Craig calculated that any garment Mrs. Clarence O. chose to flaunt ceased to look its price almost immediately.

She tottered forward on thin high heels.

'Mr. Craig! This is terrible! I can't *tell* you how *glad* I am you have got here. I am just at my wits' end to know *what* to do!'

'You called me in to do something, Mrs. Osborne. Supposing you sit down and relax.'

She affected a little shriek.

'Relax! When my jewel case with ten thousand pounds worth of jewels in it has vanished?'

She came nearer as if hoping to make him understand the enormity of her tragedy by talking into his ear. She squawked again, 'Vanished, Mr. Craig! They've gone, my lovely jewels!'

Craig lit a cigarette.

'So you told me over the phone, Mrs. Osborne,' he said patiently. 'I still think you ought to sit down.'

She stared at him out of her pale fish-like eyes for a minute and then, surprisingly obedient, sagged on to the settee.

'Yes, yes,' she muttered. 'I must be calm, you are quite right. But I am so worried, you understand that, don't you?'

'It's very understandable.'

He seated himself opposite her since she had omitted to ask him to take a chair. A bowl of mixed flowers on a small polished table stood between them.

'Can you give me any details?'

She gave him a detached smile but the crease between her scanty brows remained.

'Well,' she began, 'I was up in my bedroom at a quarter to four. I was expecting a friend — Mrs. Ashcroft — to tea, so I was finishing dressing. I had taken my jewel case from the drawer where I always keep it, and had just put on these ruby earrings when I heard her taxi.'

Craig drew at his cigarette meditatively while he eyed her ears where the jewels in them sparkled back at him. He said nothing.

After a slight pause she rattled on:

'I slipped the jewel case back into the drawer and hurried down to meet her.'

She stopped again, gulping for air, much like a goldfish which had been bodily lifted out of its bowl. He waited for her to continue talking.

'Mrs. Ashcroft had tea,' she went on. 'She left about half an hour ago. Then, suddenly, a most horrible thought came to me.' She slapped her cheek with a podgy hand to dramatize her situation. 'I remembered I hadn't locked my jewel-case away. Well, Mr. Craig, as soon as I entered my bedroom I saw the drawer was open and, just as I feared, the case had disappeared. I phoned you immediately of course. The servants have all been with me for years but as you can see, the house is full of decorators.'

Through a cloud of smoke Craig queried, 'Just one thing — as a matter of interest, you understand. What is the troupe in aid of?'

'Troupe?' Mrs. O. was startled.

Craig inclined his head towards the door.

'The personalities lined up in the hall. Someone important coming besides me? Or do you always keep them there?'

Mrs. O. looked bewildered for a second. Then she contrived to laugh.

'Oh, Mr. Craig,'
funny way you hav⟨

She leant forwa⟨
eager to impress
handling of the c⟨

'I knew you w⟨
at once. I orde⟨
until you arrive⟨

'You did?'

She nodded.

'But I'm pretty sure,' she conⁿⁱⁿᵘ
'that it is not one the servants. As I say,
they have been with me for years. It must
be one of those awful decorating men
who make such a mess.'

'Nice,' Craig observed sardonically.
'You've got it all tapped. But maybe I
should explain something before we go
any further.'

She leaned still farther forward.

'Do. Mr. Craig.'

'Technically,' Craig told her, 'you are
holding them prisoner, which the average
citizen doesn't usually appreciate and
which could get you into trouble with the
police. If I tried any funny games like
searching 'em, they would have grounds

ist you for false imprison-
ault. Could be, they'd even
nice little sum in damages.
, I'd be involved too, for aiding
tting, and personally, that isn't
run my business.'
ell!'

he outraged Mrs. Osborne sat erect;
raig reflected that 'Well' seemed to be a
favourite word of hers and thought it was
quite interesting the amount of different
shades of meaning she could get into one
syllable. She was saying angrily, 'It
doesn't appear to me that you know your
business, anyhow. I thought you looked
too inept to deal with anything serious
when you came in.'

Craig grinned without much humour.

'Have it your own way,' he said
deliberately and started for the door.

'No!'

Her yelp was an agonized cry for help.

Craig paused halfway across the room.
Mrs. Osborne clutched the arm of the
settee.

'Please forgive me. I didn't mean that. I
hardly know what I'm saying. It is

because I am so worried. I do need your
— your services. My husband is in
America at the moment but he would
loathe it if I called in the police and
— and all the publicity. He is always
telling me how careless I am and the
papers would get the story — '

She crumpled up and buried her face
in her hands. Craig waited until she had
recovered. After a few moments she
continued:

'Apart from their actual worth, my
jewels hold great sentimental value for
me.'

Craig listened to this unoriginal speech
with a smile on his lips and hand still at
the door.

'Mrs. Osborne,' he told her, 'I know it
must be very upsetting for you and I'm
afraid I'm going to upset you again. You
must go out and make your apologies all
round to that comic squad you have in
the hall, and then dismiss them. When
you have done that we'll start from
scratch.'

She raised her head.

'Must I?'

Craig nodded.

'Afraid you must. Apart from anything else, I can't take up this case until that little misunderstanding has been cleared up. I don't want any comebacks. And,' he added shrewdly, 'I shouldn't have thought you would either.'

She said slowly:

'No, of course, I don't. All right Mr. Craig, I'll do as you say.'

She sailed out into the hall, leaving the door ajar, so that Craig could hear her awkward apologies without having to give her the further indignity of having him as an audience. When the last white-coated lately-suspected individual had disappeared aggrievedly through the front door, Craig emerged from the library.

'Now,' he said briskly, 'we'll go up and take a look at your bedroom.'

The room was enormous and dripping luxury. Craig hid a smile behind his eyes as he gazed at the pink and white hangings and cushions — the stuff was everywhere — and the ultra-modern ornaments that littered the mantelpiece, dressing tables and even the wide windowsill. It was all very typically Mrs. Osborne. She was not one of the tidiest people either. Discarded clothes lay on the bed and over the backs of chairs.

She fluttered forward, waving her hands.

'I'm so sorry for all this mess, Mr. Craig. My maid has her day out and I have been so worried I haven't had time to do anything.'

Craig was sceptical of the last half of the sentence, but he trod over the thick white carpet to the dressing table where one of the small top drawers stood open.

She hovered anxiously after him.

'Everything is just as I found it.'

Craig took a fleeting glance into the drawer.

'Supposing we try a little reconstruction scene,' he suggested. 'How's your memory? If you can go over again exactly what you did when you heard this Mrs. Whosit turn up in the taxi, it might help.'

Mrs. Osborne's face screwed up in an effort of concentration.

'Now, let me see.'

Craig waited patiently.

At last she sat herself down before the mirror and started to dabble with the powder.

'Yes . . . I was just putting a last dusting of powder over my face, when I thought I heard the taxi. I paused, so.' Her hand halted in mid-air, halfway to her face. 'Then I ran to the window to see . . . '

She ran to the window.

'After that I got out my jewel-box and put these earrings on, took off my little cape that I wear over my shoulders for making up . . . Then I slipped the case into the drawer . . . so. And I went downstairs — No, wait a minute.' She stopped and turned back towards her mirror. 'I just put this curl in order first.' She patted her hair.

Craig said with a deadpan face:

'I don't think that matters, Mrs. Osborne. Just go ahead and show me how you went downstairs.'

'And into the hall to meet Mrs. Ashcroft,' she said, making for the door.

Across the berugged landing she tripped along down the wide staircase.

Craig, following slowly, caught a

glimpse of the gaunt-looking butler crossing the hall silently below them. He vanished into one of the downstairs rooms without a glance in their direction before Mrs. Osborne had reached the half-landing.

'My dear,' she cooed to the empty hall. 'That's when she arrived,' she explained to Craig over her shoulder. 'I find it easier if I talk, it comes back to me so much better.'

Craig watched while Mrs. Clarence O. flung out her arms in enthusiastic greeting of her invisible visitor. Beside the hallstand she paused and went energetically through the antics of warmly embracing Mrs. Ashcroft.

Craig, a little smile flickering round the corners of his mouth, leant his arm on the bannister. He turned slightly and cocked an eyebrow. His gaze was riveted on the hallstand with its galaxy of hats, coats and a couple of umbrellas. He crossed towards it.

'After this,' said Mrs. Osborne, enjoying herself hugely despite the fact that her jewels were still missing, 'I took Mrs.

Ashcroft into — '

'Just a minute,' Craig cut in, 'it may not be necessary to go any further.'

Mrs. Clarence O.'s eyes were round with questions.

'You mean — ?'

Craig switched the subject bewilderingly.

'Mrs. Osborne, would you say you are inclined to absent-mindedness?'

Her eyes grew rounder.

'Why . . . Well, I suppose lately with everything so rushed and living so difficult,' she decided. 'Why do you ask?'

'Because,' said Craig, 'I think in your demonstrations you may have forgotten a small but important point.'

'Have I?' She shook her head. 'I don't know what it can be . . . '

Craig didn't answer her. Instead he lifted the lid of the glove box of the hallstand. Smiling gently he slid in his hand and extracted something from the interior.

'You forgot to show me how you opened the glove box just before you showed Mrs. Ashcroft in to tea,' he said and handed over her jewel-case.

She fairly snatched it from him.

'My jewels! My precious jewels! How on earth did they get there?'

'You put them there.'

His grin grew wider at the look of utter astonishment on her face. He went on:

'Process of elimination, plus simple deduction. Want to know how it was done? First, I decided the servants could be counted out — if any of 'em wanted to pinch anything they must have had much bigger and better opportunities before now.'

She nodded and he continued:

'As for the decorating men, they're from a highly reputable firm and are as trustworthy as they come. After that, I had left only — you. And you yourself had already given me a clue.'

'I?'

'Let me finish. You thought you had put the jewel case back in your drawer. In your hurry, what you really did was to take it downstairs with you. You started to fling your arms round your friend, but the case was in the way, so, somewhat

133

absent-mindedly, you popped it into the place nearest at hand, the glove-box. Then you proceeded to forget all about it.'

Nobody could say that Mrs. Clarence Osborne didn't react. Trembling violently, she could only clutch her jewel-box more closely than ever to her heaving bosom.

'Oh, dear . . . I have been getting really bad at forgetting things lately — '

Craig grinned.

'So bad,' he said, 'that you gave me my clue without realizing it.'

'W-what clue?'

'So bad,' went on Craig urbanely, that you even thought that you'd put on your ruby earrings — '

Her hands flew in a frightened gesture to her ears. She pulled at one lobe and gazed down in dismay at the diamond earring, which glinted in the palm of her hand.

Craig laughed.

'Open the case and you'll find the rubies there.'

She hadn't waited for his suggestion. The lid was back and together they looked at the ruby earrings glowing serenely up at them from where they lay crammed into the small space amongst the rest of the jewels.

'Oh . . . ' said Mrs. Clarence O. feebly.

'Quite simple.' Craig smiled at her and caught the full weight of Mrs. Clarence O. in sagging arms as she passed out in a dead faint.

The Tenth Case:

The Girl in the Bank

It was early and a very beautiful morning: and Craig strolled peacefully along, for a change, minding his own business and rather enjoying it.

All these things considered, he was mildly annoyed when a man barged out of the London branch of the Paris Private Banking Company of La Rue et Frères and failed to look where he was going. Craig adroitly avoided a major collision but the bulging briefcase the man carried got him in his stomach.

He gazed after the offender for a second, then he turned back to the bank. Through the doors, just before meeting the briefcase, something had caught his eye. It was a girl and Craig had ceased to mind his own business for the day.

He shouldered his way through the swing doors. The expression on her face,

136

even in his lightning vision of her, had registered. She had been staring wildly at something over the other side of the counter and there had been a look of numbed horror about her. Except for her, the little bank seemed empty. It was only five minutes after opening time, so this was not so surprising as it could have been.

Craig, who never let the grass grow under his feet, summed up the girl from the doorway.

She was brunette and beautiful. No, not exactly beautiful, because she had a tip-tilted nose and her mouth was a shade too wide. On the other hand, he enjoyed just that kind of nose and the mouth meant generosity, and in any case her complexion was perfect and her lashes were the longest he had ever seen. Her light dress curved in just the right places and —

'*Mon Dieu! Mais c'est terrible! Terrible!*'

Craig came out of his dream reluctantly and moved over to her side.

'What goes on?'

137

She turned towards him. He had known, of course, that her eyes would be greeny-hazel.

'*Voyez-vous!*'

'Huh?'

He followed the movement of her agitated hand and leant across the counter.

'Well, well,' remarked Craig mildly as he took a look at the inert form slumped on the floor on the other side. He returned his gaze to the girl.

'*Parlez-vous anglais?*' he demanded hopefully in an atrocious accent.

'Yes,' she answered in her husky voice. 'I do speak English.'

He grinned at her, taking in the absurdly tiny hat perched precariously on the back of her head and looking as if it had been specially designed for her; her sheer silk-stockinged legs, which looked as if they had been specially designed for him; and her small white hands, with their carefully manicured nails clutching a substantial bundle of notes.

'Anyone at home?' he called.

There was no answer.

138

Craig went swiftly back through the swing doors and shot the bolts of the outside door with a decisive slam.

'Now,' he said, returning to the girl with a smile in his eyes. 'Suppose you try and tell me what happened — in English.'

She shook her head in lost bewilderment. 'I — I don't know . . . I just came in to pay some money into my father's account.'

'Go on. Try and remember exactly what did happen. You're a bit shocked, that's all, the feeling will wear off in a minute.'

He liked hearing her talk anyway. Her voice was warm and husky and set all kinds of vibrations thrilling through the air, and her funny little accent made it all the more charming.

She managed a tremulous smile.

'I am, as you say, a little stunned, but I will try.'

He nodded encouragingly.

She had turned her back on the counter as she spoke as if to shut away from her the frightening sight that lay on the other side. 'As I came in,' she began, 'a man rushed past me. He banged my arm — here.' She rubbed her forearm gingerly.

'Briefcase,' Craig said. Then as he caught the startled question in her eyes: 'He nearly mowed me down too, just before my entrance.'

'I see. He was very quick and I thought he must be in a great hurry about something, but then when I reached the counter, I — I saw — that — '

Her voice shook and she kept resolutely facing the swing doors.

Craig touched her shoulder for a second.

'Sit down for a minute. You'll feel better.'

She shook her head firmly.

'You must think me so stupid. But I am all right now, I do not need to sit down. It was only that it was so big a surprise.'

'I'll bet it was,' he told her. 'Have it your way, you stay standing.'

He admired her courage under the circumstances and as he made his way round the counter and got a better view of the victim he admired it even more.

The inert figure of the sandy-haired young man that lay there wasn't the sort of sight that a young and pretty girl should come across without warning just after breakfast.

He picked up the young man's wrist and let it fall again.

Blood was slowly oozing from the bullet wound just above the nape of the neck, and Craig shook his head. He left the body and glanced at the cash till. It had been emptied except for a few notes.

The girl had turned round and was facing him.

'He is dead?'

'Afraid so. You broke in on some slick work,' Craig said. 'Our friend with the briefcase must have been right on the doorstep waiting for the place to open, and once he'd been let in he didn't waste much time.'

He swung round on his heel and walked silently over to the manager's office. At the door he paused. He could see nothing through the frosted glass panel but his sixth sense yelled warnings at him.

Stepping back so that he stood clear of the door, he reached out and suddenly turned the handle; at the same time he flung the door wide. After a moment he went in.

A middle-aged man, stockily built and with a heavy moustache, stood in the middle of the room facing him. Beyond, Craig saw another door which presumably opened out into the alleyway at the back of the bank.

The stocky individual was clearly unnerved. He fingered his tie on seeing Craig and gulped once or twice before he spoke.

'Are you the police?'

'I am,' replied Craig shamelessly.

He rarely committed this harmless deception anyway, but when he did he considered it the whitest lie he ever told.

The other sat heavily down on the chair behind the desk as if his feet could no longer support him.

'I was just going to phone for you.'

Craig, leaving the connecting door wide, moved so that he commanded a view of both the man and the girl who had remained standing in the bank.

'Who are you?' he asked.

'I'm the manager . . . my name is Foster.'

'Yes? You know what's been happening out there?'

Foster licked his lips. He nodded slowly: 'Yes.'

'How?'

'I — I saw it all . . . through there — '

He broke off and indicated a grille in the wall.

Silently Craig walked over and squinted through. It commanded a full view of the counter and the outer office. He came back to the manager.

'Tell me the story from your angle.'

Foster brought out a large pocket handkerchief and blew his nose loudly before he started.

'I was in here checking over some bills of lading when I heard the commotion outside,' he explained spasmodically.

Craig, icily comparing the state of his nerves with those of the girl's in the bank, decided that he was a heavy loser.

'I looked through the grille,' continued

Foster, 'in time to see the cashier make a grab at a revolver held by a strange man. There was a shot and the cashier fell. Then the man snatched the notes out of the till and ran. There was a girl with him — '

'Girl?' queried Craig sharply.

Foster nodded.

'The one that's out there now,' he answered, and then as Craig said nothing, he went on: 'She swept up some more notes that were lying on the counter and was about to follow her accomplice when you came in.'

Craig frowned.

'Only you and your cashier here?'

'That's all. We are just a small office, open for the benefit of our Parisian customers travelling to and from London. And we do quite a lot of business with the Embassy of course.'

'What was the cashier's name?'

'Horton,' replied Foster with a certain deliberation. 'James Horton.'

Craig regarded him narrowly.

'Why didn't you make yourself known when I came in?'

Foster was having trouble with the fit of his collar again.

'How was I to know you were the police?' he objected. His tone grew slightly aggressive. 'And for all I knew the girl might have had a gun too.'

'And wouldn't that have been just too bad.'

Craig drew out his cigarette case, selected a cigarette. Foster didn't answer. Craig's lighter flared and over its bright flame he noticed that the girl had moved nearer to the office door. He dragged deeply at his cigarette and let the smoke trickle through his nostrils, then he looked blandly at Foster.

'So,' he said coldly, 'you sat tight in here and watched your cashier being shot.'

Foster began to excuse himself blusteringly.

'It all happened so quickly,' he protested. 'I was stunned by the shock. Besides, that man was a killer. He might — I mean — I thought maybe — '

He stumbled over his words into silence under Craig's sardonic eye.

'You thought he might get you too,' Craig finished for him. He turned abruptly and walked over to the door. 'Come here for a minute, will you,' he called to the girl.

She came in slowly and stood still in front of the desk. She took a quick look at Foster and then glanced at Craig but she said nothing.

Craig guessed she had probably overheard some of the conversation but his face was expressionless as he told her:

'Your story doesn't quite match up with his.'

Still she was silent and he picked up the telephone receiver and started dialling.

'What are you going to do?' she asked.

He quirked an eyebrow at her.

'The case seems to have become a little complicated,' he answered. 'I'm calling the police.'

Foster raised his head and shot him a lightning glance.

'Police?' he said quickly, 'I thought — '

Craig smiled gently. He said: 'I'm afraid I didn't quite tell you the truth.'

The other drew in a whistling breath and got to his feet.

'I shouldn't touch that phone if I were you,' he said slowly. And Craig's smile merely widened humourlessly as he found himself staring into an aggressive-looking automatic.

'Shouldn't I?' he drawled lazily. But there was not much laziness about the way his brain was working

Foster thrust his face forward.

'No, Mr. Smartie,' he said menacingly.

He leant over with a smooth movement to remove the instrument from Craig's grasp and the next moment a perfect torrent of French poured into his — and Craig's — bemused ears. And something heavy whistled through the air.

Foster gave an agonized grunt as the paperweight caught him behind the ear. He dropped the telephone and took a staggering step backwards, recovered, and turned in a white fury upon the girl.

'You little — !'

In a flash Craig moved in and crashed a right hook into Foster's stomach. The man's jaw sagged and he crumpled up with the breath knocked out of him. Craig's other relentless fist slammed against his jaw.

Over Foster's prone body Craig grinned at the girl.

'I never before,' he said, 'met a girl who hit anything she aimed at hitting.'

She smiled back at him. Her white even teeth were nice, he thought. In fact, he found everything about her nice.

'I am very glad I was an exception,' she was saying.

He looked at her.

'You're darned right, you're an exception,' he told her. They were interrupted by sounds from the outer world. Craig cocked his head.

'Somebody wants to come in.'

The banging on the front doors grew more insistent. He stooped and swept up Foster's gun from where it lay beside its now peaceful owner.

'Here,' he said handing it to her. 'Hang on to this until I get back. I'm pretty sure he won't wake up for quite a time yet, but just in case.'

He left her on guard and went to slide

back the bolts. An irate figure on the step greeted him.

'What's going on here?' he demanded.

Craig took in the other's neat appearance.

'If you're the manager,' he said, 'you're late.'

'What the devil's that got — ' The newcomer broke off as he caught the expression on Craig's face. 'I am the manager,' he said soberly. 'I've been delayed by a business appointment. Is anything wrong?'

Craig said:

'Not now. Except there is quite a chunk of money missing from your till and two bodies are making the place look untidy.'

'Good God! Are you the police? For heaven's sake, man, tell me what's happened!'

Craig told him, shortly and concisely. When he had finished, the manager said gravely:

'Poor Manning — that was the cashier's real name. What a ghastly business. I'll get through to the police at once.'

An hour later, when the police had taken over, Craig ushered the girl through the swing doors into the sunlit street.

'How about some coffee? There's a small but select joint I know not far from here, where all the tables are for two.'

Sitting opposite her and watching her sip coffee, he began to consider her all over again and decided he had been right about her in the first place. She was lovely.

'Just as a matter of interest, what is your name?'

She took a deep breath.

'Simone Thérése Marie Antoinette Lamont.'

'I'll settle for Simone. What's your job — or don't you?'

'Don't?'

'Have one.'

Her face lit up as she smiled.

'Yes, I have a job. I help my father. But he does not really need me. It is — what you call it — a stop-gap.'

Craig eyed her speculatively. He said thoughtfully:

'Maybe you've gathered my line of business?'

She nodded.

'My secretary,' he said, 'sacked me last week. Went off to get married. Could you use the job?'

She stared at him.

'Do you really mean it?'

'You'll find that one way and another I always mean it.'

'What would I have to do?'

'Keep the petty cash straight, answer the phone, brush off clients who think I'm in business just to pick their chestnuts out of the fire and get my fingers burned, answer letters and generally give the office tone with that 'Nuits d'Amour' perfume you're wearing. And,' he added, 'sling a nifty paperweight when occasion demands.'

She laughed shyly.

'It is nice of you to feel you can trust me to do all that.'

He said:

'I knew you were all right the moment I set foot inside that bank — '

'The story that horrible man told you,

you didn't believe it?'

'Not a word of it.'

'How — why?'

Craig told her:

'The way he described it. The cashier would have been shot from the front — I'd already seen he must have been shot from behind.'

'How stupid of me! But what was his idea, telling you I was mixed up in it?'

'Playing for time. He had heard me bolt the doors after his pal got away with part of the loot. He knew it wouldn't be long before someone started banging to be let in and while I opened the doors he would have been able to duck out the back way.'

He glanced down at the table as he finished speaking.

'Pretty hands you've got,' he told her.

She too looked down, and then back at him. Her eyes were smiling into his.

'Thank you,' she said.

'That's how I knew when I first saw you that you weren't mixed up in the hold-up.'

She looked puzzled.

'Process of deduction,' Craig told her. 'To which you will have to accustom yourself. If you had been a stick-up girl you would have been wearing gloves.'

The Eleventh Case:

The Face in the Photograph

Simone's head appeared round the frosted glass door with NAT CRAIG written on it.

'Lady Dawlish to see you.' As he raised his eyes from the newspaper he had been peaceably reading, she smiled and reminded him, 'She had an appointment.'

Craig sighed.

'I remember.'

She said: 'I'll show her in.'

Lady Dawlish was definitely attractive. In her early thirties, Craig decided. She sat down opposite him and placed an envelope on the desk and eyed him thoughtfully.

'Mr. Craig,' she began in a low, well-modulated voice, 'I — I find it very difficult, coming to you. Don't misunderstand me,' she said quickly as Craig raised an eyebrow. 'It is just that — well,

154

anything I tell you must be in strictest confidence — '

Craig interrupted her with a grin.

'Lady Dawlish,' he said gently, 'I don't know what your idea of a private dick is, but I assure you I have the most peculiar stories brought into my office, and they are always in the strictest confidence. It's my job.'

'Yes, yes, of course,' she said hurriedly. 'You see, I am being blackmailed.'

Craig nodded.

'Tell me about it.'

'I am being blackmailed,' she said, 'with a photograph that was taken before I met my husband — Sir Gregory Dawlish, you know.'

Craig knew. Sir Gregory was an old soldier possessed of rigid ideals, so rumour had it, and an equally rigid family background.

'It was a photograph of this man and — and myself. It happened at a party in Monte Carlo. We were young and a little foolish. I — I suppose you had better see the print he sent me.'

She picked up the envelope and slit the

top with a nicely manicured finger and slid the print over to him.

It was the kind of photograph that could be interpreted several ways. From the most broadminded view it didn't look too good. At the worst, it was a damnably compromising picture. The sort of light-hearted snap, in fact, that a blackmailer could, and apparently was, making hay with.

Craig had a shrewd notion, what was more, that Sir Gregory was the type who would think the worst.

She said, 'The really horrible part is, this man threatens to send a print to my husband — and say it was taken *after* our marriage.'

Craig nodded grimly.

'Naturally he will play his card for all it's worth. How much have you paid him so far?'

'A thousand.'

'What is his name?'

'Ronnie Meadows. He lives off Half Moon Street.'

She had done fairly well up to now but at this point her composure began to sag.

'Mr. Craig, will you be able to do something? I can't go on much longer — it's destroying me. I get no sleep and — and I love my husband.'

'I'll do what I can. Just now I want some more details.'

'Anything,' she whispered.

'When is he seeing you again for money?'

'Tomorrow night. I told him I couldn't possibly pay but he said he'd give me a month in which to find it. That is, if I pay him a hundred tomorrow. I suppose,' she added in a defeated voice, 'if I could buy the negative off him that would stop the whole ghastly business. But I couldn't possibly raise five hundred — that's what he wants for it. Not without my husband suspecting.'

Craig didn't tell her what he was thinking. Instead he said, 'You can't settle with a blackmailer by paying. There are only two ways of dealing with him. One is, face the music and go into court against him — '

'I couldn't. Besides myself it would affect my husband.'

Craig flicked the edge of the photo with his thumbnail.

'I know you won't do that,' he said. 'The other only way is to outsmart him, which is exactly what I am going to try.'

'If only you can.'

'I think I can.' His voice was quiet and just what she needed. 'But I want a few more facts about Meadows.'

When he had the information he required and she had left, he returned to his favourite position and lit a cigarette and made one or two phone calls.

About twenty minutes later he shoved his head round the door.

'Got any society magazines in the file out there?' he called to Simone.

She looked up from her typewriter.

'Do you want them all?'

Craig nodded.

He had flipped through quite a few back numbers of the glossies before he found what he wanted. He eyed the photograph between the pages with an increasing interest until, looking at the picture, he dialled Lady Dawlish's number.

'Craig speaking,' he said when she came to the phone. 'Have your husband and Meadows ever met?'

'No, never. It's doubtful if they have ever even seen each other.'

'Good. What you have to do first is tell Meadows you have managed to get hold of five hundred and you are willing to buy the negative off him — '

'Yes, but — '

'Fix to meet him at — say, Baker Street Station tomorrow evening at six o'clock.' Craig swept on, ignoring her interruptions. 'Tell him you can't risk seeing him elsewhere. And he is to be there with the negative, don't forget that. Phone me when you've arranged it.'

He clicked down the receiver before she could argue.

She came on the line about an hour later.

'It is all right,' she told him. 'I rang Meadows and said what you told me. He is going to meet me at Baker Street tomorrow. But what are you going to do?'

'You'll have the money,' Craig said. 'In one pound notes.'

'But — '

Craig smiled bleakly into the mouth-piece.

'Don't worry. I'll let you have it in good time. When he turns up bluff him into taking you back to his flat. Think you can manage that?'

'How?'

'Tell him you feel faint. That would look natural under the circumstances.'

She started to interrupt him again but he anticipated her query.

'Do as I ask and leave the rest to me — and don't worry more than you can help.'

And he hung up.

Whistling quietly to himself Craig picked up the glossy magazine and flipped through it again until he came to a particular page. Then he went off to pay a visit to a certain well-known shop off Leicester Square. When he had finished his business there, he decided to call it a day, and went in search of a bar.

★   ★   ★

It was six-thirty the following evening when Ronnie Meadows stuck his latchkey into the lock of his front door. He turned, smiling blandly at the woman who stood just behind him in the dimly lighted passage.

'Come in, my dear.' He was a smooth character. Smooth hair, smooth eyes, smooth voice. Ronnie held open the door that opened into his cosy little bachelor sitting room.

'In here.'

She walked past him and stood staring about her. He switched on a table lamp. The room was shadowed and intimate. She had half expected Craig to be there waiting for her. She had done as he had asked and had no idea what game she could play from now on.

'Do you feel better?' Ronnie asked her solicitously. 'You had better sit down. I'll mix you a drink.'

She remained standing, staring round the room.

'I don't want a drink,' she said.

'But, my dear,' Ronnie smiled at her silkily, 'you felt ill, don't you remember?'

161

He came nearer. 'You know, this is really quite like old times, isn't it?'

She looked up at that, apprehension in her eyes. Craig or no Craig, she would have to do something. She picked up the bulging attaché case that she had brought with her and placed it on the table.

'You wanted this,' she said icily. 'Hadn't you better open it?'

He regarded her a moment, smiling.

'As you say.'

As the lid of the case snapped back the heavy curtain behind him moved as if a window was open behind it.

'Gregory — !'

It was Lady Dawlish who spoke, her voice a low gasp. Ronnie swung round on his heel.

'Dawlish!' His voice cracked. 'My God, how did you — ?'

' 'Forgive the intrusion' is, I believe, the conventional apology,' remarked the newcomer. Lady Dawlish stared at him, then abruptly she turned away.

'My dear, it is quite all right. I know all about this blackmailer — ' the lip under the moustache curled and the soft tone grew stern, 'and his photograph. So you see, he can't threaten you any more. Even if he still had the means with which to do so,' he added significantly.

There was a fraction of a second's apprehensive silence in the shadowy room and then Ronnie's voice, quiet and more menacingly smooth than ever:

'Just what do you mean by that highly insinuating remark?'

'Merely this.' The response matched Meadows in calmness but there was a hint of contempt there also. 'If you don't hand over the negative now, I shall shoot you down like the rat you are!'

At the sight of the ugly automatic that had suddenly appeared in his hand, Ronnie's jaw sagged and some of the debonair air went from his voice.

'You wouldn't dare.'

'Wouldn't 1?'

'I'll see you in — ' began the other blusteringly. He broke off as the automatic moved slightly and the light caught its dull surface, sending back a sombre blue-black gleam. He shrugged. 'Okay,' he capitulated. 'Here it is.'

Lady Dawlish was there first. She put out her hand and snatched it swiftly, tore it into pieces, and thrust them into her handbag.

'All right, my dear, I think we can quite safely leave this young blackguard to his own devices now.' The other looked across at Meadows, who had thrown a veiled glance towards the open attaché case on the table, and he smiled. He said, 'I was nearly forgetting. You may keep that as a little memento. It is only perfectly harmless stage money.'

'You — !' Ronnie Meadows lunged forward, which proved to be his biggest mistake that night. It was almost as if such a move had been anticipated, because a punch that seemed to start from nowhere exploded on the point of his chin. Ronnie Meadows proceeded to take up a considerable amount of floor-space.

Lady Dawlish didn't speak until she was in the taxi. She took the cigarette that was offered her thankfully. She inhaled gratefully.

'How can I ever thank you enough?'

Craig grinned slowly at her.

'Very easily,' he said. He began to remove the iron grey wig and moustache. She looked at him questioningly.

'Just don't mention it to Scotland Yard,' he told her. 'They might take a poor view of my methods. They are never very understanding about such things as skeleton keys, illegal entry and impersonation.'

She laughed too.

'For a moment I thought you *were* my husband. That is, until you spoke.'

'When I saw his picture, I thought I might get away with it in a bad light.'

'He might have switched on the centre light.'

'I took the precaution of removing the bulb before you arrived.' He was taking an envelope from his pocket. 'By the way, you had better burn these prints with the remains of the negative.'

She caught her breath as she took them from him.

'Prints? I never thought of that.'

'I went over his flat with a fine tooth-comb. I guessed he'd run a few prints off it before he parted with the negative, so he could pick up the threads any time he ran a little short of cash, and go on blackmailing you.'

The Twelfth Case:

The Suspicious Husband

Craig came into his office and landed his hat on the peg, first throw. Simone looked up from her typewriter at his pleased grin. His grin widened as he met her gaze.

'One mystery I'll never solve,' he told her, 'is how you manage to look the way you do and business-like all at the same time.'

She laughed and said in her huskily French accent:

'Two cheques from satisfied clients to be acknowledged this morning. Oh, and there is a man waiting to see you.'

She gave a nod towards the outer office.

'Any idea what he wants?'

She shook her head.

'He would not give his name. In fact,' she said, a slight frown crossing her face, 'he seemed quite offended I did not recognize him.'

'Any reason why you should?'

She continued to look puzzled.

'I have never seen him before. Yet his face does seem familiar somehow.'

'This could need looking into.'

Lighting a cigarette, Craig went into the next room.

He, too, at once experienced the sensation there was something familiar about the man who rose to greet him.

'Good morning, Mr. Craig.'

From the way he said it, it was obvious the other fully expected to be recognized at that. A split second after he opened his mouth, Craig recalled who he was. His light blue eyes had not reproduced very well in the newspaper photographs, but there was no mistaking the high cheek-bones and the heavy moustache.

It was Henry Dewhurst, whose wife, Margaret, had been found dead in her flat a few days previously. It looked like a murder job, and Dewhurst's picture had appeared alongside hers in the national press.

According to the reports, he had discovered his wife on returning home late one evening. The suggestion was she had interrupted a burglar who had effectively silenced her.

Craig tapped the ash off his cigarette and said:

'What can I do for you?'

The other clasped and unclasped the handle of his umbrella spasmodically. His voice was somewhat high-pitched.

'It's about my wife,' he began. 'I've had about as much as I can take of this business. People looking at me sideways, the police snooping around at all hours — ' He broke off and added, appealingly, 'Could I help it if some thief broke into the flat and — ?'

'Take it easy,' Craig interrupted him. 'Just tell me what you think I can do about it.'

The other blinked. Then he said:

'Find the murderer — that's what you've got to do. The police never will. Never. And I can't spend the rest of my life under this terrible shadow.'

Craig recollected that, apart from his

alibi, which had sounded pretty cast-iron, Dewhurst and his wife had been married ten years and all the evidence showed they'd been happy together.

'Bit of a tough assignment,' he shrugged. 'What do you expect me to dig up that the Scotland Yard boys have missed up on?'

The other looked round the room cautiously, then leaned forward confidentially.

'I haven't told them everything,' he said in a low voice.

'That was wrong of you,' Craig chided him carefully. 'Very wrong. Why not?'

The other eyed him for a moment. Then:

'Because I'm not sure. Yet. I don't want to get myself mixed up in libel or anything like that.' Craig's raised eyebrow seemed to encourage him and he proceeded with increased confidence. 'I thought if I told you what I knew maybe we could work together. And you could help me deal with the police, too, if they make themselves a nuisance.'

'It's not only the police who make

themselves a nuisance,' Craig said. 'But never mind. Are you trying to tell me,' he went on, 'you have an idea who it was bumped off your wife?'

'I can't be sure,' of course,' Dewhurst pursed his lips. 'But I have my suspicions.'

'Are you going to keep them to yourself,' Craig asked him, 'or spill them to me? Strictest confidence, naturally.' And he smiled at him genially.

Dewhurst hesitated, took a nervous gulp of air, and said:

'It's Hector Bruton, my wife's brother. He always sponged on her. He lives in the same block of flats and he was for ever hanging round my place seeing what he could cadge.'

Craig gave him a narrowed gaze through a cloud of tobacco smoke.

'What motive would he have for killing the goose that lays the golden egg?' he asked quietly.

The other made an impatient movement.

'Supposing they quarrelled and he lost his temper? He's a bad-tempered blighter when things don't go his way. Oh, I admit I don't like him. But it's not only that. I've got a feeling he did it.'

Craig was staring out of the window with a far-away look. Then he turned back to Dewhurst.

'All right,' he said. 'I'll take the case. I'd like to look over your flat, for a start.'

'Could you come round this evening, say about seven?'

'Suits me,' Craig nodded. 'Give my secretary the address on your way out. And, by the way,' he added, 'you fix up with her about the fee.'

The other man's light eyes rested on him for a moment, then he nodded and opened the door.

It closed behind him and Craig heard Simone's French accent nailing him down to a not unreasonable retainer.

After Dewhurst had gone, Craig put his head round the door.

'Doing anything later that you couldn't stand up?'

'I can tell him I am working at the office,' she smiled at him. 'Where do we have to go?'

'Where our latest client hangs out,' Craig told her. 'Only we'll arrive a little earlier than he expects.'

'Where are you going now?' He had taken his hat.

'Heart-to-heart with a character name of Hector Bruton,' he told her and pulled the brim over one eye.

Hector Bruton added up to be well-groomed, middle-aged and with quite a taste in whisky. Over his drink Craig told him he was investigating the death of Margaret Dewhurst and what light, if any, could he throw on the case?

Bruton fiddled with his glass and talked a lot without saying anything until Craig got a little tired of it and shot at him, point blank:

'Would it be true you owed her money?'

The other's glass-twirling stopped for the briefest moment. He answered easily:

'In a sense you could say I did. Margaret helped me out of a tight corner once or twice. But, frankly, I regarded the money more as a gift than a loan.'

'Her husband? How did you get on with him?'

Again the glass-twirling act was halted for only a moment.

'Never saw much of him,' the other said. 'We keep our cars at the same garage, and sometimes exchanged a few words there. That's all. Oh — ' He broke off as if remembering something. 'I was forgetting. Day after the funeral it was, he did ask me up to his flat for a drink. He seemed grateful for someone to talk to.'

And that was about all Craig could drag out of him.

A little later he was making his way thoughtfully towards the lift, then something made him turn on his heel and go swiftly back. He bent to the letter-flap. It was Bruton getting on the phone that had caught his ear. Craig smiled thinly to himself.

A few minutes later he was outside Dewhurst's flat where Simone, as arranged, awaited him.

Simone saw the grim lines round his mouth, but made no comment.

Dewhurst was visibly surprised to see

them and muttered something about the appointment being at seven. In the sitting room, his self-possession regained, he said excitedly:

'I've got something to show you, Mr. Craig. Something that will settle this, once and for all.' Craig eyed him stonily, and the other pointed to a crowbar on the table. 'I found that,' he said, 'in Bruton's car round at the garage this evening. It's got traces of blood and hair on it.'

Craig glanced at it.

'You mean it's that blunt instrument business that killed your wife?'

Dewhurst nodded triumphantly.

'Obviously. And I found it in Bruton's car.'

'I heard you the first time,' Craig said.

'What are you going to do about it?'

Ignoring the question, Craig turned to Simone, who was looking at him somewhat wide-eyed.

'Buzz Scotland Yard,' he told her. 'You see,' to Dewhurst, 'they tapped the wire and listened in on you and Bruton chatting a few minutes ago. So they know it was the two of you who slugged your wife. Maybe she wasn't going to pay over your share of the profits from some racket you were working, or something. Then you got scared Bruton would squeak, so you planned to pin it on him first.'

Dewhurst muttered something that sounded somewhat unfriendly and reached for the crowbar.

As his finger touched it, Simone, with an exclamation in her excitable French, shoved the table against him, hard. It was while he was gasping for breath that Craig's fist slammed home.

'Do I really phone?' Simone asked him as he grinned at her. 'I mean, if the police tapped the wire, they'll be on their way.'

'They'll be as surprised to hear about all this as our Mr. Dewhurst.' She raised a questioning eyebrow at him as she dialled. 'Just a fast one I put over for his benefit,' he explained. 'You see, as I left Bruton's flat I heard him phoning Dewhurst and asking him plenty. It was that tipped me off they were in this together.'

The Thirteenth Case:

The Knightsbridge March Murder

There was no lift. Craig and Simone were on their way out of the old-fashioned block of flats in Knightsbridge and as they went down the linoleum-covered stairs a rush of cold air came up to greet them from the ground floor.

It was late afternoon, and the snow was still falling. In spite of the weather Craig was feeling pretty much on top of the world. For one thing, it at last looked as though he was going to clean up the case involving the client he had just left. Secondly, Simone, with her husky little French accent, gave him a glow a London winter could not chill.

They had reached the first floor when the door of one of the flats was flung open and a somewhat wild-eyed woman shot out in front of them. The woman had a large camel-hair dressing-gown wrapped round her and her feet thrust into a pair of fleecy-lined bedroom slippers. Seeing them, she drew back.

'I'm so sorry.' She sounded distraught, as if not wanting to say anything but not being able to help herself. 'I — I heard footsteps.'

Craig quirked an eyebrow but seemed disinclined to move. He waited politely, hoping for something more to follow, and the woman said:

'I thought maybe you were the police.'

The eyebrow remained raised and not a muscle of his face moved.

'What's wrong?'

The woman's eyes flickered from him to Simone and returned to him.

'It's my uncle.'

'What's the matter, has he absconded with the family silver?'

'He's dead.'

Craig eyed her thoughtfully. 'Accident? Suicide? Or what?'

She put out her hand to steady herself against the doorpost. 'I'm afraid it's murder. That was why I was expecting the police. We just phoned them.'

'Let's take a look.'

Without demurring, she led them inside and a tall broad-shouldered man with striking good looks, momentarily marred by the worried frown that creased his forehead, stepped into the hall from another room.

The woman shut the front door.

'Janet,' the man's voice held a trace of annoyance, 'I do wish you'd go and lie down and leave this to me.'

'It's all right, dear. I am perfectly steady now.' The woman turned to Craig. 'This is my husband.'

'My name is Bellton. I suppose you have come about this terrible business. Janet dear, do go and do as I say.'

Mrs. Bellton ignored his plea; instead she turned into a room on the left of the hall. Bellton looked at Craig, lifting his shoulders a little, and sighed before following her.

It was a pleasant room decorated in buff and blue with cream walls and the remnants of a small fire in the grate. Slumped in one of the buff-coloured easy chairs was the figure of an elderly man.

There was a spindle-legged table at his elbow and littered on its shining surface were stamp albums and a great number of stamp catalogues. Another larger album had slipped from his knee on to the floor. Craig took in the scene. It was fairly obvious the old man had been engrossed in his album when he had been struck from behind with a heavy instrument.

Bellton was telling him something:

'My wife's uncle, Mr. March, was a well-known philatelist.'

Craig murmured:

'I rather got that he was keen on stamps myself. To your knowledge has anything been touched?'

Bellton shook his head.

'I know nothing has,' he said positively. 'There are only my wife and myself in the flat and neither of us have moved anything at all.'

'Tell me what you know.' Craig applied the flame of his lighter to a cigarette.

There was a strangled sob. Mrs. Bellton, at the door, was staring at the still figure. Her husband was at her side immediately.

'This is only upsetting you and you can't do any good.'

'Poor Uncle,' she moaned. But she allowed him to lead her to the door. 'I'll go,' she said turning towards him. 'I'll lie down for a bit.'

'Much wiser,' he said sympathetically. When he had watched her progress across the hall to her own room he turned to Craig. 'My wife is only just recovering from a serious illness which makes it so frightful for her — '

Craig said:

'At the risk of appearing callous, it was pretty frightful for him too.' He nodded towards the huddled body in the easy chair. He continued, 'Where was she when this happened?'

'Sleeping. She's been asleep all the afternoon and didn't hear a thing. Thank heavens,' he added passing his hand lightly and wearily across his brow. 'Otherwise the thief might have attacked her too.'

'So you know it's a thief?'

Bellton laughed shortly. He said, 'Who else could it have been?'

Craig looked at him stonily.

'You mean, your guess is the thief knew about his stamp collection and was after it?'

'Of course.' There was the smallest hesitation before Bellton continued. 'Mr. March was famous for his collection of some particularly rare stamps. What's more, they have gone. They were kept in there.'

Across the room stood a writing desk. It was an attractive piece but its appearance was spoiled at the moment by the drawers gaping wide, as if they had been wrenched open violently and in a hurry.

Craig turned slowly back to Bellton, asking evenly:

'What were you doing while all this was going on?'

'I've been out at a stamp auction for Mr. March. I got back here at about four thirty and let myself in quietly, but my wife was just waking up and came out to me. It was then we found him.' Bellton rubbed his hands together energetically. 'It's terribly cold in here — do you think

182

we could have the window shut?'

Craig glanced at him curiously.

Not for the first time, it occurred to him how odd his fellow creatures were. One minute they were striking attitudes, declaring how horrible crime was at close quarters, the next they were mouthing everyday phrases as if nothing had happened.

'Bear it a bit longer,' he told Bellton shortly. He walked over the plain expensive carpet to the desk. 'In which drawer were these stamps of his kept?'

'The top one.'

Craig glanced at the open drawers. They had been turned topsy-turvy. Papers were rumpled and strewn untidily where they had been tossed aside and then back again. Thoughtfully he drew at his cigarette until the tip glowed red. He let the smoke trickle up to the ceiling in a long blue spiral column, then he left his silent contemplation of the desk and turned his attention to the window.

It was of tall proportions and was open a few inches at the bottom. Craig raised it and leaned out. Outside the fire escape wound down to the courtyard below. He became aware that Bellton was at his elbow and talking.

'Obviously where the thief came and left,' Bellton said. 'I am always afraid of fire-escapes for that reason.'

'Don't you keep the window locked?' Craig asked thoughtfully.

'Usually, yes. But I remember Mr. March trying to wipe away some of the snow from the outside just before I went out. I suppose he didn't put the catch down.'

'Couldn't have.'

Climbing out onto the iron snow-laden fire escape, Craig stood gazing down into the courtyard. It was growing dark and shadowed and yet curiously lightened by the snow that had fallen. There were footprints on the stairs but the heavy slow-falling flakes had obliterated them. Or they had been carefully blurred. Under the circumstances they didn't mean a thing.

Craig came back into the room, closing the window behind him. 'Warmer?' he asked the other solicitously.

Bellton smiled.

'It's better.'

Craig crossed to the table. There were several letters lying there and he picked them up idly, turning them over in his hand. Bellton, following him, said:

'The thief missed this, anyway.' He indicated a registered letter. 'I happen to know that it contains a stamp which has been sent to Mr. March on approval. It's worth a good deal.'

'How much?'

'At least three hundred.'

Craig tapped the ash off his cigarette on to the carpet and teetered back on to his heels. He stabbed his cigarette in Bellton's direction.

'What time does the afternoon post arrive?' he asked.

'About four thirty — '

He broke off. Simone had interrupted him with a movement. She had been watching Craig thoughtfully and now walked across to him.

'Do you think, I could have the — the window open again?' she asked in a small stifled voice. 'Some air.'

He glanced at her white face. It was too bad she had to be dragged into this at all. Except for one other occasion when she had been actively mixed up in the case, this was her first glimpse of violent death at close quarters. Still, that was what came of being a private eye's secretary.

He was about to open the window for her when a sound from outside made them all swing round. There was a key grating in the lock of the front door. The next minute, they could hear someone in the hall.

Craig shot a glance of interrogation at Bellton.

Bellton said:

'It's all right. That will only be Fuller.'

'Fuller?'

'I'd forgotten all about him during this bother,' Bellton explained. 'He is Mr. March's manservant. I'd better prepare him for the shock — '

But his words came too late. There was a movement at the half-open door and a podgy, suave figure stood framed there. His glassy eyes peered at them in mild astonishment; then, as they alighted on the inert figure, his stare widened in horror. He whispered hoarsely, 'What's happened?'

Bellton stepped forward and grasped him by the elbow.

'Steady,' he said quietly. 'This is going to be a shock — '

As he began mouthing conventional words to the newcomer, Craig turned to Simone.

'Feeling all right?'

She nodded.

'It was just for a moment.' She shuddered a little. 'What a horrible business.'

'It always is,' Craig said.

Bellton was declaring loudly:

'I think it would be better if Fuller didn't stay here. He had been in Mr. March's employ for a great many years and I'm afraid this is very painful for him. Is it all right if I take him out?'

Craig nodded assent.

Fuller was standing as one in a trance, as if he couldn't properly take in all that was going on around him. Bellton, still firmly clutching his arm, led him out.

Fuller went with the automaton-like movements of a sleepwalker.

When they had gone Simone glanced across at Craig.

She asked:

'What do you think happened?'

He was standing by the little table with his hands resting lightly on the letters and he seemed not to have heard her. He did not answer but went on smoking with a little crease etched between his straight brows. He was still in this position when Bellton re-entered.

'I'm afraid it's shaken Fuller pretty badly.'

Craig appeared to snap out of his trance. He said:

'All the same, I'd like a word with him.'

The other shrugged.

'You won't find him much help at present. But if you must, you must. He's in the kitchen.'

Fuller was sitting on a straight-backed wooden chair, leaning his arms on the table and staring into space. He looked up as Craig touched his shoulder.

'I don't want to distress you, but I

would just like an account of what happened, as you know it.'

'I know nothing,' said Fuller dully.

'Where were you this afternoon?'

'I had an important phone call from my sister. I went to meet her.'

'Where was Mr. March when you left?'

'He was in his chair.' Fuller met Craig's eye steadily. 'It was all just as usual. He was poring over his stamps like he always does — did.'

'And after your phone call? Tell me in your own words and leave me to sort it out.'

'I'll try to. As I say, my sister rang me up to say she had come to London for the day and I arranged to meet her at Piccadilly Tube Station at three o'clock. I went in to see Mr. March before I left and he was perfectly all right then, quite normal and all that. My sister was a little late arriving owing to the snow. We had tea together at the Corner House, then I saw her on her train at Charing Cross at four fifteen. I took the tube and came straight back here. And — and that's all I know.'

Craig eyed him silently.

Suddenly the manservant's head sank down on to his chest. 'Who'd want to kill Mr. March?' he choked. He looked up again. 'It must have been thieves. Someone who knew about his stamp collection.'

Craig asked him:

'Was Mrs. Bellton asleep when you went out?' He shoved a cigarette across to Fuller as he spoke. His lighter flared.

'Thanks.' The hand that took the cigarette shook badly. 'Yes, she was asleep, I imagine. She went to bed after lunch.'

Craig didn't think he'd get much more out of him.

Back in the sitting room he found Simone standing by the window and Bellton fidgeting round the room. He addressed Bellton: 'You say you telephoned the police?'

'Just before you arrived.'

Simone said, 'They have probably been held up by the snow — '

'Just a minute,' Bellton interposed suddenly, staring at Craig. '*What did you say?*'

Craig said nothing but Simone looked round in surprise.

'I said, the snow must have — ' she began, but Bellton was not taking any notice of her; he still eyed Craig keenly.

He said, his voice hard: 'Just who *are* you two? If you are not connected with the police?'

Craig smiled sunnily. 'We just happened to be passing.'

'Just — !'

Bellton took a step forward but he was interrupted by a violent ringing on the doorbell. He checked himself.

'Well, that will be the police now, anyway,' Simone said.

'Excuse me,' Bellton said and went into the hall.

The next minute two men came in with snow dripping off their overcoats and hats.

Bellton followed on their heels and after a quick side glance at Craig he waded knee-deep into his story. When he had finished, Craig drew deeply at his cigarette and what he said jarred the other as if he'd been hit by a steam-hammer.

191

'Now, why don't you give 'em the real facts? It would save us all a lot of time and I want to get home.'

The plain-clothes men stared uncomprehendingly, first at Craig, then at Bellton. The latter's jaw shot out.

'I've just told them what I told you.'

'I know,' Craig said serenely. 'That's the trouble. But don't be shy — tell 'em how smart you were really.' His voice was quiet but charged with dynamite. 'Go ahead and tell them how you went to the stamp auction — cooking up a cosy little alibi for yourself there — then you came back here.'

'You don't know what you're saying — ' Bellton's tone was shrill. There was fear in his eyes.

'Fuller was out,' Craig continued, smooth as silk. 'And you knew it. This was just the chance you had been waiting for to get your hands on those stamps while keeping yourself in the clear. *Don't move.*'

Bellton had stepped towards the door but as Craig spoke one of the plain-clothes men moved adroitly across his path. Bellton gave a hunted look round the room.

'Don't listen to him!' he cried hoarsely. 'He's crazy.'

Craig said coldly:

'You let yourself in without waking your wife, and slugged the old man. Then you popped out down the fire escape, which you thought pretty clever. It all helped to make it look like an outside job — incidentally you were much too eager to show me those footprints. Back to the front door again, but this time you took good care your wife did hear you. You wanted her with you when you found her uncle.'

The silence in the room was so acute they could almost hear the snow falling outside.

'The only snag was,' Craig went, on remorselessly, 'that just after you had killed him, the postman arrived.'

Bellton, his face ashen, slumped into a chair and moaned:

'Stop it! Stop it!'

Both plain-clothes men were at his side as Craig continued:

'You were forced to answer the postman's ring or he would have woken your wife too soon for you. You forgot him — until I spotted these letters. Then you slipped up badly. You see, you couldn't have found that registered letter on the mat — postmen have an annoying little habit of not leaving registered letters without getting a signature for them.'

The Fourteenth Case:

Shown in Red

The scene could have been a stage set.

Mrs. Frensham's study was large, high-ceilinged and mid-Victorian. The furniture, lost in the shadows, was massive. The carpet was the sort you sank in up to your ankles.

Mrs. Frensham, in contrast to all this somewhat overpowering impressiveness, was slim, attractive and dressed beautifully. She was about thirty-five and as she sat under the pool of orange light spilt by the desk reading lamp she looked fragile and lost.

It was merely a trick of light and shadow and contrast; Craig knew Mrs. Frensham to be an exceedingly capable and busy woman, interesting herself in all matters of public life and the wife of a very rich husband. Still, there was that look about her and, it seemed to him from where he stood just inside the door, that she had black smudges under her fine eyes which might have been caused by sleepless nights.

They stared at each other in silence. Behind her the French windows stood open and the heavy claret-coloured velvet curtains were drawn back, allowing a white mist that crept slowly up the dark garden from the Chelsea Embankment to eddy into the room in little ghostly fingers of vapour. The whole atmosphere of the set-up was gloomy and heavy with impending tragedy. Craig decided it was time that things brightened up a bit.

He switched on his charm and smiled.

'Good evening.'

Mrs. Frensham turned a blonde head so that the hair glinted in the light but she avoided his eyes as she spoke.

'Good evening, Mr. Craig.' Her voice was low but perfectly steady. 'I am afraid you have come unnecessarily. I no longer need your help.'

Craig hung on to his smile but his eyebrows went up the fraction of an inch.

'What made you change your mind?' he asked politely and advanced into the room. 'You didn't phone me just to hear what a private detective really sounds like. Or could it be,' he asked, 'you wanted to see what one *looked* like?'

She didn't laugh. Instead she turned the full battery of her eyes upon him.

'I have told you I no longer need your services, isn't that enough?'

He politely ignored her hinted request to go. Instead he hitched himself tranquilly up on to the corner of the desk. She watched him from where she sat swamped in the big swivel chair.

'Don't you understand?' Her voice had a pleading note in it and there was a hint of fear too. 'When I telephoned you I was frightened for myself. Now there is someone else. You can do nothing.'

Craig nodded urbanely. He was thinking suddenly of the only other occupant of the house that he had so far encountered. Mrs. Frensham's secretary. A tall girl, her honest cockney accent heavily disguised by a Mayfair drawl. The type who got around Soho dives and Chelsea taverns. So he had summed her up from his brief glimpse of her when she had shown him into the room.

He got off the desk in one swift movement and padded across the room. He opened the door with a jerk. There was no one there. Quietly he re-closed the door. The woman behind the desk sat very still, watching him with raised brows. He came back to her side with a disarming grin.

'I was just wondering if your secretary — '

'Brenda?' There was a wealth of surprise in her voice. 'Miss Green — ? Why should you think she would listen at doors?'

'It's the way my mind works,' he told her.

'She knows nothing.' It was a flat statement.

He shrugged his shoulders but showed no intention of leaving; instead he changed the subject abruptly. He decided if she was going to reveal anything at all the only method was to surprise her into it.

'Where exactly does your husband

figure in all this?'

The effect of his question was dramatic beyond expectation. Mrs. Frensham went a deathly white and he thought for a moment she was going to faint. Next, he entertained rather different thoughts as she made a grab for her expensive-looking handbag. But it wasn't a gun she pulled out.

'Take this twenty pounds and go,' she said urgently. 'Please, Mr. Craig. I realize I have caused you some trouble asking you to come here, but perhaps this will compensate you.'

Craig looked interested. In fact, he was becoming more and more interested every moment.

'Care to add a further thirty to it and I'll stick around and clean up the whole business for you.'

'No — '

He continued as if he hadn't noticed her vehement interruption: 'And a whole lot cheaper than paying blackmail.'

He heard her sharp intake of breath.

'How did you know?'

Craig smiled and pressed home the

advantage he had scored by his shot in the dark.

'Who is he? When are you seeing him again? Tonight?' He fired the questions at her like a machine gun. He wasn't expecting her answer.

'I shall never see him again. He's dead.'

Somewhere from the river a tug hooted. The note hung mournfully on the silence, a silence as heavy and enveloping as the blanket of fog sluggishly curling in through the open window. Deliberately, Craig searched in his pocket for his cigarette case. As he exhaled he thoughtfully sent a smoke-ring sailing up to the ceiling. Slowly he tilted his head back to the level of her eyes and said:

'Who killed him? You? Your secretary? Or could it be your husband?'

She gave a little cry and covered her mouth with her hand.

'No! You're not to say that. Do you hear? You're not to!'

'I asked you a question, Mrs. Frensham. If you interpret it as a statement it's not my fault. What happened?'

She shook her head desperately.

'I was being blackmailed.' She broke off, biting her lip. 'I'll tell you what I know. He — the man — was coming here tonight for more money.'

Craig said grimly:

'Go on.'

She gave a tremulous sigh.

'I'd heard about you and on the spur of the moment decided to get your help. It was while I was speaking to you on the phone that I heard him. He was out there.'

She glanced behind her at the French windows and shivered.

Craig remembered the abrupt way in which she had rung off. It was that which had intrigued him in the first place and had brought him along in a rush.

'He'd been stabbed.' Mrs. Frensham pressed her handkerchief to her lips as she recalled the horror of that moment. 'He was standing there in the window looking at me — ' Her vice broke on a hysterical note. 'There was — blood. He tried to say something, but I couldn't hear. As I moved towards him he fell. I — I dragged him across the lawn behind the shrubbery. Then I came back here and tried to think what to do.'

'And did you decide?'

She looked straight at him.

'I asked myself,' she said evenly, 'who could have murdered him. My husband's temper is — well, if he'd found out about him and — and me, there isn't any knowing what he might have done.'

'What was this man's name?'

'Harry Trannion.'

'Harry Trannion.'

Craig repeated the name. It was not an easy one to remember — a startled terrified gasp from the woman opposite him shattered his concentration.

'Harry!'

Craig followed the direction of her eyes and saw the figure in the open French windows. As they watched it sway and clutch at the heavy curtain, the figure took a staggering step into the room. Mrs. Frensham was on her feet, her face as white as the man's who had just entered. He tottered blindly towards them, machine-like, horrifyingly deliberate. His clothes were soaked with mist,

202

muddied and torn; his face, with light staring eyes glazed with the approach of death, was streaked with blood. Halfway to them he halted and moved his lips stiffly, the effort drawing painful breaths from him.

'For God's sake — !' he managed to gasp, then with a gurgling choke he pitched forward on his face. Craig was the first to reach his side. Harry Trannion had been stabbed in the back.

'He's dead now, anyway,' he told Mrs. Frensham. 'Your diagnosis was a trifle premature — must have only been unconscious. Pretty tough specimen. I wonder what became of the knife?' He straightened up. 'Take it easy.'

With a quick stride he reached Mrs. Frensham and, an arm round her waist, took her back to her chair. She was a ghastly colour, but after she had rested for a few seconds she raised her eyes.

'It's all right,' she said wanly. 'I won't faint on you or anything like that.'

He smiled tautly.

'Seeing the same man dead twice in one night is a bit of a strain. If you feel all right I'm going to call the police.'

His words had the effect of pulling her together. She clutched at his arm.

'You can't. You can't do that. My husband — they'll take my husband. Oh, can't you see? That's why I wanted you to go in the first place. I knew you'd bring the police in.' She broke off and started to sob quietly. 'I could have kept it quiet — I could have shielded Guy — '

Craig's voice became a whiplash.

'Get this, Mrs. Frensham.' His grasp tightened round her wrist. 'And get it straight. You can't shield anyone from murder. If your husband did it, then he'll have to — '

'Have to what?'

The words took them both by surprise. So did the sight of the man behind the double-barrelled shotgun.

'Have to what?' he repeated, remaining standing in the doorway.

'Guy — ' Mrs. Frensham half rose in her chair but he ignored her.

'Well?' he said to Craig. 'You're so full of good advice, young man, finish what you have to say.'

Craig, lounging on one corner of the desk swung his foot. 'Anything you like,' he acquiesced affably. 'If you did it, you'll have to swing for it.'

There was a strangled sob from Mrs. Frensham but her husband never moved a muscle. Not a trace of emotion showed on his face.

'My wife,' he said tensely, 'obviously believes I murdered this blackmailer — oh, yes, I overheard all I needed — So why do you say, 'If'? Not that I care what you think. The only thing I'm certain of is that you are not going to call in the police. You're going to get out now and I'll handle this my own way when you're gone.'

'A thing I hardly ever do,' said Craig with engaging candour, 'is argue with a double-barrelled gun.'

His cigarette was almost burning his fingers and he leaned unhurriedly over the desk and crushed it out, then he uncurled himself and stood up. 'I'll be getting along then,' he told Frensham chattily.

As he started across the room the

woman sprang out of her chair.

'Mr. Craig.' He paused for a second with raised brows. 'Mr. Craig, you won't — I mean, you won't do anything — '

And then came the third interruption.

'Did you ring?' asked Brenda Green, appearing dark and questioning behind Frensham.

Frensham started and half turned; the gun wavered in his grasp for a second and Craig jumped.

'Guy!' shrieked Mrs. Frensham as her husband went staggering back against the wall from a jab in the stomach that had all Craig's weight behind it.

'A thing I should never advise you to do,' observed Craig, slamming the door shut with his foot, 'is argue with a double-barrelled gun.'

Doubled up with his arms folded across his middle, Frensham eyed him with acute dislike and his suspicious gaze travelled across the desk where the bell-push stood close to the ashtray.

'Must have touched it when I stubbed out my cigarette,' Craig told him blandly.

Brenda Green looked bewildered.

'What is all this?' The girl came further into the room and broke off, her hand at her throat. 'My God!' she whispered. 'Who is it?'

Nobody enlightened her as she stood transfixed, staring at the dead man. Frensham turned a defeated expression towards Craig.

'All right,' he said. 'Go ahead. Call the police.'

Craig shrugged and started to back to the desk but Brenda Green was before him.

'I'll phone them.'

Craig nodded.

She sat herself down in the chair Mrs. Frensham had vacated and started to dial. She was pale but seemed to have recovered her composure except that she was fidgeting nervously with a red pencil as she put through the call.

'I'll talk,' Craig told her shortly, taking the receiver and gazing abstractedly at the blotting-pad. He said into the mouthpiece, 'Name of dead man, Trannion. Yes. It's murder and the killer is here waiting for you to collect.'

The tension that hung on the air made the room practically sizzle. The receiver clicked back into its cradle. Craig got slowly to his feet and looked deliberately at Brenda Green. She was staring desperately at the gun he held. He grinned bleakly as he read her mind.

'Better with me than with you,' he said laconically.

Brenda Green suddenly slumped into a chair, her head in her hands.

★   ★   ★

Craig said to Detective-Inspector Holt over his drink later:

'Funny how the little things give murderers away.'

The other grinned.

'I've been waiting to hear how you finally settled on the Green girl,' he admitted. 'It would make it much more simple for us if they all broke down and confessed as she did. But how did you work it out before calling us?'

'I realized Trannion must have had

somebody passing on information about Mrs. Frensham to him and who better than her secretary? Then, as she told us, when he had started to put the pressure on *her* as well as Mrs. Frensham, she decided to get rid of him. Trouble with these crooks is they never know when to stop. If Trannion had been satisfied with what he was getting out of the Frensham woman and paying Brenda her cut, he might have gone on for years.'

Craig shrugged and took a gulp from his glass.

Holt smiled.

'You still haven't told me how you pinned it on Brenda,' he said.

Craig laughed.

'Obviously Mrs. Frensham would never have contacted me if she had planned to kill Harry Trannion. Her husband could be eliminated, he owned a gun and a fiery temper and would have blown dear Harry to blazes with both barrels instead of messing about with a knife. Then Brenda gave it to me herself sure enough. Handed it me on a plate. When I was speaking to you on the phone I saw what she had scribbled on the blotting-pad. Doodled Trannion's name in red pencil so that it stood out like a neon sign — and a moment or two before she had been asking who he was.'

The Fifteenth Case:

The Swiss Cottage Swiss

The taxi skidded to an uncertain stop by the kerb, throwing up slush and snow; and Craig, who had been leaning back in the corner with his feet on the tip-seat opposite, threw aside the morning paper headlining the electricity cuts, and got out. He paid off the driver and went up the slippery steps of the large building where Reuben White had his offices.

Reuben White was a plump little man, immaculately dressed and usually sparkling with a lively wit and oozing geniality, all of which served to conceal a shrewd business brain. This morning, however, Reuben White was worried and harassed, betraying both emotions by his excitable manner. He proffered Craig an inlaid cigarette box and watched while he lit up. Then he poured forth his troubles.

Craig finally broke into the torrent of

211

words with a quiet:

'What do you expect me to do that the police can't?'

'Get my diamonds back!' replied Reuben instantly, his well-kept hands talking nineteen to the dozen. 'They were insured for ten thousand. And worth fifteen at today's prices,' he added with gloomy melancholy.

Craig smiled a little at the tragedy in his voice.

'Horrible for you.'

Reuben White's bright little eyes gleamed with fury.

'That fool of an assistant I have. It was his fault. If only he had remembered to ask me for the keys of the safe and locked the diamonds away, they would never have been stolen. Never.'

Leaning back in his chair, Craig gazed thoughtfully out on to the snowy rooftops.

'The thief must have watched you pretty closely,' he said.

The other shrugged expressively and spread his hands.

'People are always coming and going,

coming and going in my offices,' he said in the tone of one suffering a deep personal injury. 'It could be it was just a sudden temptation only. He maybe never stole anything before. I do not know.'

He dismissed the question as unimportant.

Craig smiled to himself and stood up, letting his gaze rove round the office with its large wall-safe and untidy tables littered with the various accessories of the jewellery trade. Then he came back to White.

'This clerk of yours? Symes, did you say his name was?' The other nodded. Craig went on, 'How long has he been with you?'

'Two years already. But then I still know little about him. Very little about him. I was urgently needing a clerk at the time. His testimonials were good and I took him on. I have had no trouble till now. But — ' He broke off, snuggling his large chin down into one shoulder with a curious bird-like movement. 'Who can tell?'

Said Craig softly:

'I'd like a talk with Symes.'

'Certainly,' said White with alacrity. 'But I do not think you will get much out of him.'

Reuben White was right.

Symes was cagey; he had sandy hair and a hesitant manner and Craig decided he was on negative ground and dealing with a type who would be scared easily into dumb reticence. He went to work on him cautiously, chatting about this and that, the weather, the difficulties of living and the rest. Finally he discovered Symes had a harassed wife and an ailing child. Also that his weekly pay packet from Reuben White didn't exactly need a truck to carry it home.

'What exactly did happen yesterday afternoon?' Craig asked him confidentially, at last.

Immediately the frightened look returned to Symes's eyes but he answered quickly enough.

'Well, I — I don't hardly know anything. I had expected Mr. White back from his lunch at two thirty, but he didn't come back then. It made things a bit awkward, I don't mind telling you.'

'Why was that?'

'You see, it was like this. While Mr. White was out, one of the agents with whom we're in touch came in with a wallet of diamonds.' He glanced up at Craig anxiously. 'The same diamonds that are causing all this trouble.'

Craig nodded encouragement and the other went on.

'This agent had the stones on loan as he had a client interested in them. As a matter of fact, the client had bought one, and the agent came in yesterday to return the others. Well,' the man paused and his eyes wavered, 'I had to go out on an errand soon as the agent had left and — and Mr. White hadn't come in, so — so — '

'So?'

Symes licked his lips.

'I popped them into a drawer in the desk. What else could I do? Mr. White had the keys to the safe. He won't part with them, for all I've been here two years and ought to be trusted by now.' He gulped and continued. 'I got back at twenty to three. Went straight to the drawer to get the stones but the wallet had gone.'

He stopped speaking and Craig could almost see him, under the defensive attitude he adopted, cringe mentally.

'Notice anything unusual on your way out or when you came back?' he asked in a friendly voice.

The other hesitated.

'As I went out, I did notice a man who was a stranger to me come into the building. But I don't suppose that means very much. There are generally plenty of people who pass in and out of these offices and you can't know every face.'

The defensive note was back. Craig asked him:

'Could you describe the man? Any details?'

Symes paused and appeared to give it some thought.

'Yes, I could,' he said at last. 'He wasn't very large nor yet very small. He had rather a long thin face with a little moustache, one of those swanky pencil-line moustaches I think they call them.

And he had rather a high complexion, I noticed that particularly because it didn't seem to go with a thin face. Yes,' he said thoughtfully, 'ruddy-faced, he was.'

'Notice anything else? His voice for instance? Did you hear him speak?'

Symes brightened.

'Yes, I did. Not to me he didn't speak but I overheard him ask the lift-girl if it was working and she told him it wasn't. Rather a hoarse sort of voice he had.'

And that was all Craig could dig out of him.

Thinking over Symes's evidence there wasn't a lot to go on, but Craig had his hunches. Back in his own office he gave Simone an account of the morning's happenings She smoothed back her hair and said:

'You don't think that poor little clerk had anything to do with it?'

Craig grinned at her. 'What is this?' he said to her. 'I thought you'd never seen him?'

She smiled back. 'I haven't.'

'Intuition, eh?'

'He sounds as if I should feel sorry for

him,' she said, 'But don't go by me, expect I'm wrong.'

Craig was momentarily distracted by the way her hair curled into the nape of her neck.

'You look so right, when you're wrong,' he said.

Simone smiled but she was enjoying it all the same. She told him: 'You've got work to do. Remember?'

It wasn't until they reached the street and Craig had hailed a cruising taxi that Simone asked where they were going.

'To have a heart-to-heart with Paul Delamere. We should be able to locate him fairly easily.'

'And who,' asked Simone with commendable restraint, 'is Paul Delamere? And why will he have to be located?'

'I have a hunch,' Craig sidestepped her question. 'A bell rang rather loudly when your poor little clerk chatted about the hoarse voice. Added to the rest of the description it seemed to fit an old customer of mine rather too well to be ignored. Especially as dear Paul always had an interest in precious stones, so we're going to try a few of his old haunts.'

They finally ran Delamere to earth in a bar, which was situated at the bottom of a short flight of dingy stone steps. He was leaning his elbows on the counter and glaring morosely at a row of empty glasses. His countenance brightened considerably when he saw Craig and Simone.

'How nice, how nice,' he greeted them jovially. 'Mr. Craig, it's been a long time. What are you going to have?'

'Much too long a time,' observed Craig gently. 'But drinks are on me, or has someone left you some money?'

Delamere was not embarrassed.

He rustled a wad of notes and showed a row of yellow teeth in what he fondly believed to be a smile.

'Business isn't too bad, Mr. Craig,' he said airily. 'Not too bad at all.'

He broke off and ogled Simone brazenly. She returned him an uncompromising stare and thought that Symes's description of the unknown man certainly fitted him. Voice included.

Craig was saying:

'I suppose business kept you fairly busy

round about three o'clock yesterday afternoon?'

Delamere hooked a hand round a glass of beer and handed a gin and orange to Simone with the other, then he said casually:

'Matter of fact, it did. Why do you ask, Mr. Craig?'

Craig raised his glass before replying. Then:

'Just tell me what you *were* doing?'

Delamere wiped his pencil moustache down with the back of his beringed hand. 'Funny you should ask, all the same,' he said ruminatively.

'What's so funny?'

'Because I had an appointment with a pal of mine at about that time in Swiss Cottage. Chap named Ottori. He's an exporter — '

'What would that description add up to exactly?'

'He exports things,' Delamere said a little aggrievedly, 'anything from nuts and bolts to steamrollers.'

'Diamonds too?'

There was a split second's hesitation

and Delamere managed to look really hurt.

'Now, now, Mr. Craig,' he protested hoarsely, 'don't go getting wrong ideas. I'm not saying I don't know what you're getting at — vaguely, of course — but you've got the wrong angle on me. I've given up all that sort of thing.'

'Glad to hear it.' Craig put down his glass. 'What was so funny about you having an appointment with him?'

Delamere explained.

'This chap Ottori? Swiss, he is. Joke, see? Living in Swiss Cottage, I mean.'

'Hope he'll have nothing worse to laugh off,' Craig said.

Delamere took no offence.

'You come out with the most amusing things, Mr. Craig,' he chortled.

Craig looked at him bleakly.

'I should like to pay a call on Mr. Ottori.'

Delamere obligingly wrote the name and address down on a greasy bit of paper, which he dug out of his pocket, and then waved them goodbye with the utmost equability.

'Be seeing you,' he called after them, eyeing Simone hopefully.

'I should think our Sunny-Jim is just about right there,' Craig observed as they climbed into a taxi and rattled off in the direction of Swiss Cottage.

Ottori's address turned out to be a luxuriously appointed flat in an ultra-modern block. Craig said maybe he was in the wrong business as Ottori asked them in.

The exporter of anything from nuts and bolts to steamrollers was in a helpful mood. His geniality rivalled that of Delamere, he was better dressed and his English was excellent.

'Yes, yes,' he acknowledged Craig's question. 'It is quite true. My friend Paul Delamere was here yesterday. I expect to be sending him abroad quite soon on a little buying job. He came here so that we could make the final arrangements.'

'Can you say what time he got here?'

The Swiss smiled affably and said that he could.

'Half past two. I can tell you exactly because he was punctual. I am a very punctual man, myself, and I welcome it in others. That is why I remember so clearly.'

He grinned round at them and Simone decided he looked rather like a self-satisfied and over-fed jellyfish.

'Very interesting,' murmured Craig. He was expected to say something.

The Swiss nodded into his own fat.

He added fruitily, 'I noted the time by that,' he said, indicating the chromium clock on the wall. 'My good friend Delamere stayed three quarters of an hour. At a quarter past three he left. I had somebody else calling at three fifteen.' He frowned reflectively. 'I regret to say *he* was ten minutes late.'

Craig was staring thoughtfully at the slow-moving hands of the clock as he drew on his cigarette. It was just on six.

He turned to Ottori:

'I'd like to use your phone.'

The Swiss spread his hands. 'Certainly. Go ahead.'

Craig reached across the table and pulled the telephone towards him. As he dialled he said:

'Too bad to have put you to all this trouble. Routine.'

Ottori was very agreeable.

'But I completely understand, Mr. Craig. It has not put me out at all, I assure you.'

Craig spoke into the mouthpiece.

'Give me Inspector Jackson, please.'

There was a sharp, hastily stifled exclamation from Ottori, then he said genially:

'Have I given you something useful to go on?'

'You certainly have.'

Ottori leaned forward and there was something subtly menacing about his grotesque figure bulging silently round the edge of the table. There was a glint in his eyes that caused Simone to glance apprehensively.

'Just — what?'

Craig grinned at him.

'Relax: You'll get your chance to talk your way out of it.' Into the phone: 'Jackson?'

Ottori growled, 'I don't know what you're getting at.'

Unperturbed, Craig continued to talk

to the Inspector.

'About those diamonds pinched from Reuben White. A character by the name of Paul Delamere should be able to spill quite a bit about them. And while you're picking him up you might send someone along here.' He gave the address. 'Friend of Paul's. Charming type, name of Ottori. You'll like him. Very helpful. He'll fill in any gaps in Delamere's conversation.'

Simone cried out a warning as Ottori awoke from his astonished stupor and shot out a podgy hand in an attempt to wrench the receiver from Craig's grasp. Lazily, it seemed, Craig raised the instrument and banged it hard against Ottori's jaw, and the Swiss subsided with a strangled yelp of pain.

'I told you to relax,' Craig told him equably. 'The other way somebody will only get hurt — and it won't be me.'

And he turned back to the phone.

* * *

Sometime later he and Simone were back in a bar and she was eyeing him speculatively over the rim of her glass.

'I have never heard two men implicate each other so completely as those two did,' she said.

'Delamere and Ottori? They hadn't a leg to stand on once their alibi was broken.'

She said curiously:

'But their stories, that Paul Delamere was at Ottori's Swiss Cottage Flat at the time when the diamonds were stolen from Hatton Garden, matched so well.'

Craig lit up for them both.

'Ottori,' he said slowly, passing her the glowing cigarette, 'chucked the flaw in their story slap in my face.'

'But I do not see.'

'The clock on the mantelpiece blew their alibi to bits.'

'But I do not at all see what an ordinary clock could tell you. Except the time?'

Craig said:

'But it was not an ordinary clock. It was an electric clock.' He laughed at the growing bewilderment on her face. 'Swiss Cottage was one of the spots yesterday where the current was cut between two and four. So it couldn't have been pointing to two thirty or even three fifteen, as so carefully planted by Ottori. And if you're going to ask why crooks make such stupid mistakes, that is one little mystery even yours truly can't solve.'

THE END

DR. MORELLE MEETS MURDER
A CASE FOR DR. MORELLE
DR. MORELLE'S CASEBOOK
DR. MORELLE INVESTIGATES
DR. MORELLE INTERVENES
SEND FOR DR. MORELLE
DR. MORELLE ELUCIDATES
DR. MORELLE MARCHES ON
MEET JIMMY STRANGE
ENTER JIMMY STRANGE
DEPARTMENT OF SPOOKS
NEW CASES FOR DR. MORELLE
THE RETURN OF
SHERLOCK HOLMES

We do hope that you have enjoyed reading this large print book.

Did you know that all of our titles are available for purchase?

We publish a wide range of high quality large print books including:
Romances, Mysteries, Classics
General Fiction
Non Fiction and Westerns

Special interest titles available in large print are:
The Little Oxford Dictionary
Music Book, Song Book
Hymn Book, Service Book

Also available from us courtesy of Oxford University Press:
Young Readers' Dictionary
(large print edition)
Young Readers' Thesaurus
(large print edition)

For further information or a free brochure, please contact us at:
Ulverscroft Large Print Books Ltd.,
The Green, Bradgate Road, Anstey,
Leicester, LE7 7FU, England.
Tel: (00 44) **0116 236 4325**
Fax: (00 44) **0116 234 0205**

GUILTY AS CHARGED

Philip E. High

A self-confessed murderer recounts the events that led up to an apparently unprovoked attack; a gruesome murder scene holds nasty surprises for the investigating officers; a man makes what amounts to a deal with the devil — and pays the price; caught up in events beyond his control, a bit-part player in a wider drama has his guardian angel to thank for his survival . . . These, and other stories of the strange and unaccountable, make up this collection from author Philip E. High.

THE CLARRINGTON HERITAGE

Ardath Mayhar

When Marise Dering marries Ben Clarrington and moves into the old mansion where the rest of the Clarringtons live, she's ordered to keep out of the closed-off sections of the third floor — but is not told why. It is only later that she learns the sinister family secrets . . . but has she been told all of them? As the family members begin perishing in odd and horrifying circumstances, Marise must try to uncover all the secrets of the Clarrington heritage . . .

THE GLASS ARROW

Gerald Verner

West Dorling is a quiet, remote village. So what brings three men to live thereabouts at practically the same time? None of them seems to pursue any professional employment, yet they live in some style. When a local learns their secret and threatens blackmail, the three meet to discuss this threat. But on arrival, two of them find the other lying dead, shot through the heart by a glass arrow. Before long a second has died in the same manner. Who is the mysterious archer and why use *glass* arrows . . . ?

JIMMY LAVENDER
CHICAGO DETECTIVE

Vincent Starrett

Jimmy Lavender — Chicago Detective. The name conjures images of gangland murders, Al Capone and illegal bootleg whiskey, but Lavender has more in common with Sherlock Holmes. In some of his most baffling cases, Lavender comes up against such brain-twisters as a marble fountain statue that seemingly comes to life and walks by night; a fiancé who goes missing on the eve of his wedding; a missing sack of uncut diamonds; and murder, robbery, and sudden death on the high seas!